Derby Divas

By

Kathi Daley

This book is dedicated to my daughter-in-law, Brennen, who is the best daughter a woman could ever have.

I also want to thank my team of advance readers for taking time out of their busy lives to help me launch each new book with a special thanks to Bruce for help with the techy stuff.

And, as always, love and thanks to my sister Christy for her time, encouragement, unwavering support, and valuable feedback. I also want to thank Carrie, Cristin, and Danny for the Facebook shares, Ricky for the webpage, Rick for the info regarding classic car shows, Randy Ladenheim-Gil for the editing, and, last but not least, my super-husband Ken for allowing me time to write by taking care of everything else.

Special thanks to all my Facebook friends, who show their support by sharing their opinions and encouragement. I'd like to give a special shout out to SUPER FANS:

Amy Brantley
April Pierce Schilling
Betty Solomon
Charlene Cobleigh Soreff
Cindy Loving
Dawn Frazier
Debbie Steele
Karen Borowski
Kari Frazier
Kathi Detamore
Kayla Moore
Lisa Kelley
Marijo Wheeler
Marissa Yip Young
Mary Brown
Mary Fulwiler
Michelle St James
Robin Driscol
Robyn Konopka
Ruth Anne Dingwell
Ruth Nixon
Vivian Shane

Books by Kathi Daley

Zoe Donovan Cozy Mystery:

Halloween Hijinks

The Trouble With Turkeys

Christmas Crazy

Cupid's Curse

Big Bunny Bump-off

Beach Blanket Barbie

Maui Madness

Derby Divas

Haunted Hamlet

Turkeys, Tuxes, and Tabbies

Christmas Cozy

Alaskan Alliance

Shamrock Shenanigans – March 2015

Paradise Lake Cozy Mystery:

Pumpkins in Paradise

Snowmen in Paradise

Bikinis in Paradise

Christmas in Paradise

Puppies in Paradise – February 2015

Whales and Tails Cozy Mystery:

Romeow and Juliet – January 2015

Road to Christmas Romance:

Road to Christmas Past

Chapter 1

Monday, July 7

"I can't believe Zak wanted to sit next to Levi," I complained to my best friend, Ellie Davis. We had just spent two wonderful if not hectic weeks in Maui, where we'd participated in a treasure hunt, solved a murder, and made several new friends.

"Maybe he wanted to take a break from the crazy woman who broke his heart," Ellie answered without looking up from the book she was reading. Her long brown hair shielded her face so that I couldn't see her expression, but I was pretty sure she was as disgusted with me as Zak must be.

"I'm not crazy," I defended myself as I crossed my legs up under my body in the large and plush seat provided by the private jet Zak had hired for our flight home.

"The most eligible bachelor on the planet just asked you to marry him and you said no." Ellie turned and looked at me.

"I didn't say no. I just didn't say yes."

Ellie rolled her eyes.

"He took me by surprise," I tried to explain. "I know I should have said yes, but I froze."

"So unfreeze," Ellie counseled. "Get out of your seat and walk down the aisle and tell that wonderful man who loves you more than life itself that you would be honored to be his wife."

I can't actually see my own face, but I'm certain I look like a fox trapped in a briar bush by a pack of angry dogs. I snuggled my dog Charlie to my chest and hid my face in his furry neck. For any of you who may not know me, I am a twenty-five-year-old animal rescue worker who apparently is a total idiot when it comes to committed relationships. I've been dating my ex-nemesis and current love of my life for nine months. After two glorious weeks in Maui, the most perfect man on earth, Zak Zimmerman, asked me to marry him. I guess you can tell by the cryptic conversation with my best friend and soon-to-be roommate that I didn't handle things as well as I might have. You see, in spite of my many fabulous qualities, I tend to have a teensy problem with commitment. I either avoid it altogether or latch on so tight to those I've already committed to that I smother them with possessiveness and jealousy. My name is Zoe Donovan and I'm a complete and total mess.

"Exactly how mad do you think Zak is?" I asked.

"Any normal man with reasonable emotions would be both hurt and furious, but knowing Zak, he's probably just taking a moment to give you the space you asked for."

I knew Ellie was right. After I failed to respond to Zak's heartfelt declaration of love, he had very sweetly let me off the hook by apologizing for springing the whole thing on me in such a spontaneous manner. He'd told me that he knew I wasn't ready and should have waited and promised that things were okay between us. We'd walked back to the beach house we were borrowing from Zak's friend and, although it was still early, Zak claimed he was tired and wanted to turn in. He kissed me gently, but I couldn't help but notice the hurt in his eyes. By the time I joined him, he was fast asleep, and when I woke this morning, he was already up and busily packing our gear in the limo that would take us to the airport.

I looked across toward the back of the jet where Zak and Levi were watching some dumb movie and laughing like they were having the time of their lives. What is it with men and slap-shot comedy? Since when is getting kicked in your private parts and squirting mayonnaise out of your nose something to roll on the floor laughing about?

I sighed. Something was definitely wrong with me. I know, as an ovarian member of the human race, I should find such antics childish and inane, but to be honest, projectile mayo is exactly something I would normally find hilarious. Maybe I contracted some tropical disease while on the Islands that robbed me of my good judgment and sense of humor. We *had* spent a lot of time diving at fairly significant depths in our attempt to find buried treasure. Maybe I was suffering the effects of nitrogen narcosis. Then again, maybe I was possessed.

"Do you believe in ghosts?" I asked Ellie, who had returned her attention to her book.

"Ghosts?"

"Yeah, you know, spirits from the undead who come to you while you sleep and possess your body, making you do things you would otherwise never have done?"

"No," Ellie answered definitively.

"But there are odd things that happen to people. Remember that show we saw on cable where the old woman was believed to be possessed by her dead husband, which was causing her to do all sorts of weird things she normally wouldn't do?"

Ellie put her book down and looked at me. "You aren't possessed. You're scared. It's normal to be scared when we face major life changes. We all go through it, and I suppose there are times when listening to the little voice in our heads that tell us that agreeing to something we only think we want isn't the right decision."

"So it was really smart of me to take a step back rather than accepting Zak's proposal right away?"

"No."

"But you just said . . ."

"I wasn't talking about you. Zak is great and you should marry him. Now." Ellie waved her hand in the air to indicate I should be on my way. "Do not pass go, do not collect two hundred dollars. Just do it."

"You were talking about yourself," I realized.

Ellie looked back at her book and pretended to read, but I could see the moisture forming in the corners of her eyes. Now I really felt bad. Here I was jibber-jabbering about my so-called love crisis when poor Ellie so recently had been dumped by her own fiancé. To make matters worse, I suspected she had slept with the third member of our best-friend trio, Levi Denton, while Zak and I were chasing a killer on Oahu.

I'd tried to gently broach what I knew would be a sensitive topic after I'd witnessed Ellie sneaking out of Levi's room when we returned early to the oceanfront house Zak's friend had let us borrow, but

Ellie refused to speak of the matter. I could tell that she wanted to forget the whole thing had ever happened, and I was honoring her request for the time being.

"I'm sorry, Ellie." I wound the fingers of my right hand through the free hand in her lap. "Really. I've been thoughtless and insensitive. I know you've been dealing with your own stuff. Do you hate me?"

Ellie smiled and set her book aside once again. "I don't hate you. I'm sorry too. I know this is hard for you. I've been insensitive. I guess I'm angrier about everything that happened with Rob than I care to admit, and as far as the other . . ."

"You're scared."

"Of course I'm scared," she whispered. "I ruined everything."

"Ruined everything how?" I asked.

Ellie glanced at Zak and Levi, neither of whom was paying the least attention to our conversation.

"You know how I feel about Levi, but nothing has changed. He doesn't want children and I do. We can never have anything more than friendship. I understand that, and I value the relationship we have more than I can say. It kills me to think that one night of moonlight and tequila may have destroyed what it has taken us a lifetime to create."

"You feel like you crossed a line you can't uncross?" I guessed.

"It was worse than crossing a line. The whole thing was a total nightmare."

"It was bad?"

Ellie paused and looked directly at me. "It was worse than bad. It was wonderful."

"Oh." Given their difference in life goals, I could see how wonderful could be worse than bad. With bad, you simply laughed it off and moved on. But with wonderful . . . wonderful could haunt you the rest of your life.

I squeezed Ellie's hand in a show of support. "You and I and Levi have a relationship that is strong enough to withstand anything," I assured her. "I know things feel awkward now, but give it some time. Things will get better. You'll meet a new guy who wants a family and Levi will meet a girl who doesn't, and you'll both wonder what drew you to each other in the first place."

Ellie looked at me like I'd lost my mind. Even I had to admit that my attempt at comforting her was lame.

"Rob is a jerk." I tried for just the right amount of best-friend outrage as I changed the subject back to her ex-fiancé. I guess I figured that outrage was an easier emotion to deal with than regret.

"He's not a jerk." Ellie smiled at my less than successful attempt to cheer her up.

"Yeah, I guess not. But your landlady . . ." I growled. "What a witch to lease your apartment right out from under you."

Ellie actually laughed. We both knew it hadn't been her landlady's fault that Ellie had forgotten to inform her that her plans had changed and she wouldn't be moving out of her apartment at the end of the month as planned. Unfortunately, the woman had been very efficient in renting the unit while we were in Hawaii.

"My landlady is a wonderful woman who just did what I'd asked her to do," Ellie pointed out.

"Although my oversight has put me in an awkward position. I'm never going to find another apartment I can afford on my own."

"Don't worry," I said, trying to comfort the woman who had been like a sister to me my entire life. "We'll get you moved out of your old apartment and into the boathouse."

"What about Zak? Are you going to give up on him altogether?"

"No," I said. "But once he's speaking to me again, we can stay at his place on the nights when we . . ." I blushed. "You'll see," I continued without completing my previous thought, "it will be fun to be roomies for a while."

"Fun?"

"Sure, why not?" Charlie leaped down from my lap to join Zak and Levi, so I adjusted my body so that I was sitting sideways. "It'll be like the slumber parties we had when we were kids."

"We aren't kids anymore," Ellie said.

"Speak for yourself," I challenged her. "I love slumber parties. I think I even have some peppermint schnapps in the back of a cupboard somewhere. Remember that holiday party when we drank way too much of the stuff and spent the rest of the night prank calling Levi?"

"He didn't speak to us for a month," Ellie reminded me.

"That was because we sent Penelope Waters over to his house." I laughed.

"That was mean and you know it."

"Yeah," I had to admit, "it really was."

Penelope had had the biggest crush on Levi all through our freshman year of high school. She'd followed him everywhere, even changing many of her classes to coincide with his. During the aforementioned slumber party, Ellie and I had called Penelope and told her that Levi was secretly in love with her and she should go over to his house and refuse to take no for an answer until he agreed to take her to the winter formal. Looking back, it really was a terrible thing to do. Levi hadn't wanted to hurt Penelope's feelings, so he actually took her to the dance even though he was the most popular boy in school and could have taken anyone he wanted.

I watched Ellie as she watched Levi. He was mimicking the antics of the men-children on the screen as Zak laughed at their outrageous deeds. In spite of Levi's completely juvenile behavior, I knew that Ellie must be hurting. Problem was that I really wasn't sure what I could say that would make her feel better. She wasn't wrong in her assessment that a long-term intimate relationship between Levi and herself was most likely not in the cards. Levi was the sweetest guy on the planet—next to Zak, of course— and would make someone a wonderful boyfriend, but they simply wanted different things in life. I knew that the quickest way for them both to get past this moment was to move on to someone else. Now I just needed to figure out a *someone else* to fix Ellie up with.

Chapter 2

Tuesday, July 8

Tuesday mornings meant gathering in the back room of Rosie's Café for the weekly Ashton Falls Events Committee meeting. Levi, Ellie, and I were all members, along with county liaison Willa Walton, my dad and representative of the volunteer firefighters Hank Donovan, town librarian Hazel Hampton, preschool owner Tawny Upton, local theater arts coordinator Gilda Reynolds, and our newest recruit, Paul Iverson, who had taken over the summer camp program after Frank Valdez was arrested for attempting to rob the bank last April.

"Welcome back." My dad scratched Charlie behind the ears after he gave me a hug and a kiss on the forehead. We were the first members to arrive at the restaurant. "Where's Zak?"

Zak wasn't a formal member of the committee, but more often than not he attended meetings when he was in town.

"He decided to go visit Scooter," I informed him.

Scooter Sherwood is a precocious nine-year-old who had managed to get himself into quite a lot of trouble after his mother died and his dad checked out emotionally. The fact that he'd turned into the town terror wasn't really surprising since he was left to his own devices much of the day. In an effort to help me out of a potentially sticky situation regarding a dog bite a few months earlier, Zak had agreed to babysit Scooter while his dad was out of town. The two had bonded, and a relationship forged on mutual respect and admiration had been born. Once Scooter's dad had returned to town, he'd packed Scooter up and moved him to Kansas to live with his grandparents. Zak and Scooter had stayed in touch, so it wasn't totally a surprise when Zak announced that as long as he had a private jet at his disposal, he was going to drop us off and then head to Kansas for a few days to see how Scooter was getting along.

"How is Scooter doing?" Dad asked.

"I think he's doing okay," I answered. "He misses Zak and isn't thrilled to be living with his grandparents, but they seem to be good people who only want the best for him. At the very least, I'm sure they provide a stable environment, while his father didn't."

"Seems odd Zak would take off so soon after getting back from your trip to the Islands," Dad commented.

I suspected that Zak was giving us both some space but didn't say as much. "We ended up coming home from Hawaii earlier than expected, so he had use of the jet for a few more days. I guess he figured he was already packed, so why not. I know he bought a ton of souvenirs for Scooter the day we were in Lahaina, so he probably figured it would be more fun to deliver them in person than to mail them."

"Yeah, I guess that makes sense. Do you want to come by the house later to say hi to your mom and Harper?"

"I'd like that. I actually bought a lot of stuff for Harper the day we went shopping as well. I need to go to the Zoo and check in with Jeremy," I said, referring to the wild and domestic animal control and rehabilitation shelter I run. "Maybe I can come by around five?"

"Five should be fine. I'll let your mom know to expect you."

"Have you moved back to the guesthouse?" I wondered.

Long story short: my mom got pregnant with me when she was still a teenager. She decided she wasn't ready to be a mom, so she gave me to my dad to raise. She came back into our lives a year ago and became pregnant with my baby sister Harper after a single night of passion with the man she had never stopped loving. They bought a property with a main house and a guesthouse. The parents wanted to raise Harper together, but neither were quite ready to commit to anything permanent, so the current lodging provides the opportunity for my mom and Harper to live in the main house, while my dad lives nearby, in the guesthouse. During the final weeks of her pregnancy, my dad had moved into the guest room of the main house to help Mom out, and as of a couple of weeks ago, the guest bedroom had been where he remained. I really hoped that my dad moving into the main house was a step toward my ultimate dream of my parents married, but while I was away in Hawaii, I'd learned that my dad intended to move back to the guesthouse.

"Actually, I thought we could talk about the situation when you come by tonight."

"Yeah, I guess this isn't the best place for the discussion," I said.

I waved to Hazel, who had come in with Willa, and settled Charlie at my feet when we took our seats and waited for the others to trickle in. While everyone on the committee had a specific need for the funds raised by our monthly events, it was up to Willa to ensure that all the income from our efforts was properly accounted for and distributed.

"Are Levi and Ellie coming?" Willa asked.

"As far as I know," I answered as Gilda walked into the room with Tawny.

"I'm so glad you came back early," Gilda said in greeting. "We could use additional input on a discussion we had last week about the feasibility of having the men and women compete separately in the derby."

"Separately?" I asked.

"As you know, initially the derby was an all-male event consisting of sixteen men who were divided into two groups of eight in the qualifying rounds," Gilda explained. "The final four left running in each group were then entered into the final round. The last car running in the final eight was declared the winner. That always worked out quite well. Then, two years ago, Pandora Parker convinced the committee that she should be allowed to enter if she chose to do so. Not only did Pandora win the Derby last year, ruffling quite a few feathers in the process, but with her victory, we've had five additional women register for the event this year, giving us a total of six. Six!"

"That's good," I commented. I knew that although Pandora was new to the derby competition, she'd been attending the classic car show for years. She owned a classic car parts and restoration shop in her hometown and attended the shows both to promote her services and acquire used parts for her business.

"Not really," Gilda countered. "Several of the men dropped out of the tournament because they didn't care to compete with women, so we have ten men competing, for a total of sixteen entrants. As you know, we're using a new field this year since the fairgrounds were unavailable. The field should accommodate six to seven vehicles at a time. The prior discussion centered on creating two distinct divisions, a women's and a men's, instead of dividing the pool into coed divisions. If we segregate the men from the women, we could place all six women in a single group, eliminating the need for a qualifying round, with the men in two groups of five, with the final three from each group moving on to the final round. The committee discussed it at length, but I'm afraid the vote was split."

Levi walked in and took a seat on the other side of my dad. "Vote was split concerning what?" he asked.

Gilda filled him in as Ellie joined us, sitting down in the empty chair between Gilda and Hazel.

"I don't think that segregating the men from the women is going to go over well at all with the women," I pointed out. "I realize that some of the men were tweaked that we opened the event to women, but in my opinion they'll just have to learn to deal with the fact that they were beat by a girl. It seems like the only fair way to handle sixteen entries is to randomly divide the cars into groups for the qualifying rounds, as we've always done."

"Levi?" Gilda asked.

"I don't see the problem with having a men's tournament and a women's tournament. They separate men and women in most other sports."

"I guess it's up to you." Willa looked at Ellie. "Levi, Gilda, Paul, and I feel we should have two separate divisions and Zoe, Hank, Hazel, and Tawny feel we should let the women compete with the men. Four to four."

Ellie glanced at Levi, who winked at her. "I say let the men and women compete in the same derby," she decided.

I smiled and Levi frowned.

"Okay." Willa sighed. "Since the venue we have is smaller than the one we've used in the past, we'll need to divide the drivers into smaller groups for the qualifying rounds. I'm thinking four groups of four, with the final car from each group continuing on to the finals. On to other business. Tawny, how are you doing with the food for the event?"

I watched Levi and Ellie as Tawny gave her report. Levi was making an effort to make eye contact with Ellie, but she was steadfastly ignoring him. I knew there was tension between them due to the events of the past few days, but I really hoped that any awkwardness would dissipate as we returned to our regular lives. The three of us had been friends for such a long time. I hated to see anything interfere with that.

"Is that okay with you, Zoe?" Willa asked.

"I'm sorry, I guess I missed that. Is what okay?"

"Can you take over the scheduling of the qualifying groups?" Willa repeated.

"Yeah," I agreed. "I'd be happy to help out with that."

"Excellent. I know that both Pandora and Boomer Stevenson are planning to show up tomorrow. Since Pandora is the unofficial spokesperson for the women and Boomer is generally considered to be the top-rated male, perhaps you can share our decision with each of them."

"Sure," I said. "Are they staying in the Ashton Falls Motor Inn?"

"I believe they are. You can leave a message with the desk clerk to have them phone you when they get in."

"I'll stop by and chat with the clerk when we're done here," I promised.

"Excellent." Willa turned to my dad. "Hank, are you all dialed in for the classic car parade?"

"Everything is set," Dad assured Willa. "The cars will cruise down Main Street on Thursday, Friday, and Saturday evenings, beginning at eight o'clock. Each car has been assigned a spot in the park during the day so that spectators can come by at their leisure, view the cars, and chat with the owners. The food vendors will be organized on the south end of the park near the gazebo. I know that Tawny has arranged for tables to be set up in the center to create a food-court type setting."

"And the chili cook-off?" Willa asked Paul.

"All set. We have eight entrants. The competition will be held on Friday. Entrants will be allowed to set up any time after seven a.m., and judging will be at four. Samples will be available to the public once the winner has been selected."

"Wonderful," Willa stated. "I volunteered to be in charge of organizing the sock hop, and Hazel and Gilda have agreed to help me with the actual event.

Everything is set for Saturday night. We were able to get a fantastic band known for their renditions of favorites from the fifties and sixties, and I've managed to put together a reliable decorating party for the community center so that the six of you will be free to oversee the other events. Ellie, if you could help Tawny with the food, and Paul, if you will help Hank to oversee cruise night, Levi can assist Zoe with the final round of the demolition derby. Friday and Saturday will be busy days for all of us, so I'm hoping we can all meet at around seven?"

Everyone agreed that seven was fine. Ellie volunteered to bring coffee and Tawny said she'd provide the doughnuts.

"Okay, it seems like we're in good shape for the weekend," Willa said, beginning to wrap things up. "The cars should begin arriving tomorrow and the first event is scheduled for Thursday. Thursday will be a light day, with only the classic car parade. Is there anything we need to address in the meantime?"

"Are we doing a poker run this year?" I asked.

"Yes, on Friday afternoon," Willa informed the group. "There will be five stations. Paul, Hank, Gilda, Hazel, and I will each man a station. Tawny and Ellie will be busy with the snack bar and Zoe and Levi will be busy with the derby, so I haven't assigned you any other tasks associated with the event. Is there anything else?"

No one said anything.

"Okay, the meeting is adjourned."

Ellie pulled me aside as I stood up to leave.

"I need to talk to you. Do you have time today?"

I really didn't.

"Of course," I answered anyway. "I really should head over to the Zoo and check in with Jeremy, and I promised my dad I'd come by after work to visit with Mom and Harper for a while. Maybe you can come over later? Say seven?"

"Make it seven-thirty. The Beach Hut closes at seven, and I really should let Kelly go home early since she's been covering for me for two weeks." Kelly is Ellie's assistant at the Beach Hut and the woman responsible for keeping the place running so that Ellie could go on vacation and volunteer for the classic car event. "How about I bring dinner and a bottle of wine?"

"Sounds perfect."

Zoe's Zoo, so named by Zak when he purchased the facility from the county, is an animal shelter dedicated to the rescue, rehabilitation, and relocation of wild and domestic animals. My assistants, Jeremy Fisher, Tiffany Middleton, and Bobby Evans, have an impressive track record when it comes to finding the perfect home for each pet. Along with our night crew, brothers Tank and Gunnar Rivers, we make a good team. Jeremy had been in charge while I was away, and although I had initially been nervous about being away for so long, based on the daily conversations I'd had with him and Tiffany, it seemed like everything had been handled perfectly during my absence.

"I'm back," I announced as I walked through the front door.

The lobby was empty.

"Is anyone here?" I called.

"Back here," Tiffany answered.

I walked down the hall to find Tiffany and our veterinarian, Scott Walden, standing over a dog lying on the exam table.

"I'm afraid Bruno came down with an intestinal infection," Tiffany informed me.

Bruno, a boxer, had been with us for about a month.

"He hasn't been able to keep anything down for a couple of days, so Scott is going to put him on an IV. He's been sedated."

I walked over to the table and looked at the much-too-thin dog. He was unconscious but seemed to be breathing comfortably.

"Is he going to be okay?" I asked.

"He should be," Scott answered. "We'll need to keep him sedated until we can get some fluids in him. I've shown Tiffany what to do, and I'll stop by on my way home from the clinic to check on his progress. If things go well, we'll reduce his level of sedation and start him on a limited diet tomorrow. How was your trip?"

"It was really . . ." I searched for the right word, "interesting."

"Tiffany told me about the murder investigation and treasure hunt. Do you even know what it means to take a vacation? You're supposed to do things like lay on the beach and maybe read a book or two."

I shrugged. "You know me. I like to be in the middle of things."

Scott laughed. "Did you at least find the treasure you were looking for?"

"Not yet," I admitted. "I guess these things take times. Years even. We found some really awesome artifacts and our friend Malie is working with her uncle to try to figure out the discrepancy between the artifacts we found and the location where the boat they were supposed to be on went down. If they find anything significant, we can always go back so we can be in on the find."

"It sounds like a fascinating project. I never learned to dive, but your treasure hunt is causing me to reconsider the idea," Scott informed me. "I really should get going, but maybe we can discuss it in more depth in the future."

"I'd love to."

"Call me if there's any change in Bruno's vitals." Scott gathered his things.

"I will."

"Are we still on for tonight?" He glanced at Tiffany.

"I'll meet you at six-thirty, as planned."

I noticed Tiffany's grin as Scott walked away.

"So are the two of you dating?" I asked. I knew that Tiffany had been working up the courage to ask Scott out for quite some time.

"I'm not sure I'd classify it as dating, but I asked him to go to a movie with me a couple of days ago and we really had a good time. We're meeting for dinner tonight. So far, the whole thing has been very platonic, but I'm hoping that our friendship will evolve as we spend time together."

"Scott is a nice guy. I think the two of you will make a good couple. I'm glad you finally got up the nerve to ask him out."

"Believe me, it wasn't easy. I almost changed my mind, but Jeremy was here, and he brought up the subject of the movie, making my asking Scott to go a little easier."

"Where is Jeremy?" I asked.

"Stray-dog call. He should be back in a few minutes."

I made sure that the sides on the table on which the dog was lying were raised and locked before we left the room. He was out cold, but I didn't want to risk him rolling off. Once the IV was removed, we'd move him to a dog bed in the recovery room.

"Anything I need to know before I dig into that pile of mail and paperwork on my desk?"

"Not specifically. The report from the surprise inspection we had on Friday is on the top of the mail. Not to toot our own horn, but we nailed it."

"I knew you guys would." I smiled.

Actually, when Jeremy first told me about the inspection, I had been terrified, but he'd managed to convince me that he could handle it and, obviously, he had.

"Did you ever find out why we were targeted so soon?"

"Not really," Tiffany answered. "The woman who came by said it was standard procedure, but Jeremy thinks there was more to it. Either way, she was very impressed with our entire operation."

"Wonderful. I'm proud of the job you and Jeremy did while I was away."

Tiffany smiled.

"By the way, I really want to thank you again for staying at the boathouse to take care of Marlow and Spade. I know Marlow can be a handful and it was a lot to ask."

"Are you kidding? I should be thanking you for allowing me to spend two weeks in your lakefront home. It was like taking a vacation of my own, which was great because I can't afford to go away."

"I noticed the kitty condo in the corner of the bedroom."

"I know you're concerned about space and I'll take it back to my mom's if you want, but Marlow loves it, and it seems to have taken care of the laundry issue."

While I was in Hawaii, Tiffany had told me Marlow liked to make a game out of emptying the hamper and spreading her clothes all over the house. He often did that to me as well, and she'd speculated that he was bored while he was home alone all day. Although he had a buddy in the house, Spade is a lazy cat who likes to sleep, while Marlow likes to play. Tiffany's mom had the kitty condo in her garage from when Tiffany'd had a cat as a child, so she'd offered to bring it over and give it a try.

"He does seem to like it," I said. "He loves to climb to the top and swat at that stuffed bird you hung from the ceiling. It looks like Ellie is going to be moving in with me for a while, so I'm not sure I'll be able to keep it for the long run, but I'd love to keep it for now."

"Ellie is moving in with you?"

"Yeah. She has to be out of her apartment by the end of the month, so I offered to let her stay with me until she can find her own place."

"Wow, your boathouse is great, but it's not really designed for two."

"We're going to put most of her stuff in storage, but she'll need a place to put her clothes and personal items. It's going to be tight, but I'm not sure Ellie is emotionally ready to find a permanent place to relocate. Besides, I can always stay with Zak if it gets to be *too* cozy."

"Yeah, I know Zak has plenty of room. I thought he might come in with you this morning. We talked about building another couple of outdoor runs before you left. He mentioned coming by to take measurements when you returned from your trip."

"Zak went to Kansas to visit Scooter," I informed Tiffany. "I'm sure he'll be by when he gets back." I looked at the mess on my desk. "It looks like I have a mountain of mail to deal with. Can you send Jeremy in to see me when he returns?"

"Yeah, no problem. I'll be exercising the dogs if you need me."

I hoped I hadn't been too abrupt about ending the conversation with Tiffany, but I didn't want to talk about Zak. Besides, a mountain of mail really was an understatement. I supposed I could have had Jeremy open the mail and deal with what he could, but in spite of the excellent job he was doing, I couldn't quite bring myself to give up that amount of control. Not that I'm a control freak, because I'm not. Usually. Okay, maybe I am, but only about things I care about. The Zoo is an extension of my love for our four-legged friends and I take what I do very seriously.

"You're back." Sixteen-year-old Bobby Evans stuck his head in the door.

"I am." I smiled. "I heard you have a new addition to your family."

"I do." Bobby grinned. "Want to see her?"

"Sure." I set aside the pile of bills I was sorting and followed Bobby out of the building. "Where did you find her?" I asked as we walked out the front door.

"Craigslist. I couldn't believe the guy was letting her go so cheap. I called right away and ended up bringing her home that very night."

"She's a real beaut," I commented. "I thought you said you had your heart set on black."

"I did, but when I saw this pretty little lady, I knew how rad white could be as well."

"She's quite a bit older than you were looking for," I pointed out.

"Yeah, but she's got good bones. She needs a little work, but I think she'll do what I need her to do. Want to try her out?"

"I'd love to, but I have a mountain of work. Maybe tomorrow? Are your parents happy with your choice?"

"Not really." Bobby gently caressed his thirty-five-year-old find. "But love at first sight is love at first sight. I'm sure you get that."

Actually, I did.

"I know my mom is pretty disappointed by my choice, but I'm pretty sure my dad gets it. He's already hinting around that he might want to borrow her sometime. Plus there's the whole cool factor."

"Yeah, she's cool all right. Congratulations. I'm sure the two of you will be very happy together."

I left Bobby ogling his new toy while I returned to my office. I'll admit that I envied him. There's something really special about your first. I know I still remember mine with warmth and affection.

"Did you see Bobby's new car?" Jeremy asked as we passed in the hall.

"I did. He was lucky to find a Mustang he could afford."

"She has the 302 v8 engine, and it has pretty low miles, considering. I took her for a drive the other day and fell in love."

"The maintenance is going to cost him a fortune," I pointed out.

Suddenly I realized that I sounded like my father.

"But totally worth it," I added.

"Yeah, she's pretty sweet. Makes me wish I'd gone for love over practicality when I bought my ride. Of course, Bobby has a lot more free time than I do, and I have a feeling he's going to be spending a lot of time under the hood of the old gal."

"Speaking of old gals, did Winifred Spears ever decide what she was going to do with Bella?"

Winifred was a longtime resident of Ashton Falls who had been gifted on her eighty-fifth birthday with a condo in an assisted living community by her son Randolph. Winifred wasn't thrilled with the gift and made sure that everyone knew it, but after a fall on the ice last winter while she shoveled her walk, she had finally decided to go along with the wishes of her children and make the move. The problem was that the community she was moving into didn't allow dogs over forty pounds, and Bella, a golden retriever/Newfoundland mix, weighed over a hundred. Winifred was determined not to move until she found the perfect placement for Bella and was dragging her feet, creating a fair amount of frustration and tension between Winnie and her children.

"I found Bella a home that even Winnie thinks is a perfect match for her precious baby." Jeremy beamed.

"Ethan Carlton." I suggested the name of the man I'd had in mind for Bella.

"Better. Zak Zimmerman."

"My Zak?" I was stunned that Jeremy had even talked to Zak. He'd never mentioned adopting Bella.

"I called him this morning and he said he'd be happy to provide Bella with a home. Winnie is thrilled that she's going to live in a mansion on the beach, and Zak even promised to let her come and visit from time to time."

Zak was going to be a perfect parent for the large and active dog, but it hurt that he'd never even discussed it with me before agreeing. Of course, we weren't married or even engaged, and he knew me well enough to know that I'd be thrilled he was helping out with the Winnie-and-Bella situation.

"I hope it's okay that I called him directly." Jeremy looked uncertain. "Winnie's son came in first thing this morning and wanted an answer by noon or he was going to take matters into his own hands and find Bella a home himself. He's in town to move Winnie to her new condo this afternoon. You were in the meeting when I thought of Zak."

"Of course it's okay," I assured Jeremy. "Zak will be perfect. He's been lonely since Lambda died, and I've been thinking of talking to him about another dog. I don't know why I didn't think of Bella. She's a beautiful dog with lots of energy to do the things with Zak that Lambda never could."

Jeremy sighed in relief. "I'm glad it's okay. Winnie's son can be very pushy, and I have to admit I was feeling desperate. I knew Winnie would be crushed if we couldn't find the perfect home for Bella, and her son wasn't giving me much time. You listed Zak's cell as one of your emergency numbers, so I went ahead and took a chance and called him directly. I didn't realize he was out of town, though. Winnie's son wants Bella picked up by three o'clock today. Zak said he was going to call you about taking delivery."

I looked at my phone. I'd turned it off during the meeting. I powered on and saw that I had both a text and a voice mail from Zak. "Yeah, he did call, but I had my phone turned off," I answered. "I'll head over and pick Bella up in a little while. I'm sure Charlie will be thrilled to have the company."

Charlie lifted his head at the sound of his name.

"By the way, excellent job with the inspection. The woman from the county seemed quite taken with your knowledge and level of expertise."

Jeremy smiled. "That's not all she was taken with. We're going out this weekend."

Terrific. The last thing I needed was a messy love affair between Jeremy and a county representative who could shut us down with a single stroke of her pen.

Jeremy must have noticed the look of despair on my face.

"Don't worry. We aren't dating," he assured me. "I know the rule about mixing business and pleasure. Vivian is a nice woman my mother's age who happens to like classic cars. Morgan and I are going to show her around. I assure you that I'll be on my best behavior. By the way, I wanted to let you know that the mysterious animal deaths we were dealing with while you were away have stopped completely since they isolated the water supply your dad told Salinger about."

"That's good. Did they find the source of the contamination?" I wondered. While I'd been in Hawaii, several animals had died or become sick as a result of contaminated groundwater. My dad and Jeremy had helped track down the source of the toxins.

"Not yet, but Salinger assures me he's working on it. My guess is that one of the cabins in the area is being used as a meth lab, but it will be hard to figure out which one without searching each and every one unless someone slips up and brings attention to themselves. Guess we'll just have to keep an eye out for any more deaths."

"I'm going to call Zak and then head over to Winnie's to pick up Bella. My phone is on now, so call me if anything comes up."

Chapter 3

I felt bad for Winnie. I understood why her children were concerned about her living alone in a house that required shoveling snow in the winter and yard work in the summer, but Winnie was an independent soul who probably wouldn't love living in a structured community. I was glad that Jeremy had thought of asking Zak whether he was interested in being Bella's new human. They really would be perfect for each other and I couldn't believe I hadn't thought of it myself. Zak hadn't answered his cell when I called, but I'd left a voice mail letting him know that I was picking up Bella and would be happy to keep her at my place until he returned.

"I guess you're here for Bella." Winnie had tears running down her cheeks when she opened the door. I had to bite my lip to keep from shedding a few tears of my own.

"I can come back later if you need more time to say good-bye," I offered. I love my job, but situations like this are the worst.

"Now is good." Her son walked up behind Winnie with Bella on a leash.

"Let's talk on the porch," Winnie suggested.

I stepped aside as Winnie and Bella joined me outdoors. It felt like my heart was breaking as Winnie hugged Bella, but I couldn't think of anything I could do or say that would make this easier for her. Saying good-bye to a beloved pet was never easy.

"Zak is excited to have Bella come to live with him," I tried. "He's going to take good care of her."

"I know he will." Winnie smiled through her tears. "I can't bear saying good-bye, but Bella is a large dog who needs a big yard and someone to walk her. My new condo doesn't have much of a yard at all."

"Jeremy said you could have a small dog. Have you thought about adopting another dog that wouldn't need much exercise?"

Winnie's eyes lit up. "Do you have a dog like that?"

I considered the question. Winnie would need a small dog who was well behaved and wouldn't require vigorous exercise. An older dog would be perfect for the elderly woman, although I wouldn't want to pair her with a dog so old as to have health issues. I had six dogs under twenty pounds currently at the shelter. Three were super-hyper and two had a tendency to bark at everything that moved. The sixth dog might work, but none seemed quite right.

"What about a cat?" I asked. "I have a beautiful longhair tabby named Sheba. She's sweet and gentle. Her owner recently passed away, and I've been looking for just the right placement for her. She likes to sit on your lap and rock away the afternoon but isn't real tolerant of other animals or small children."

"I don't have other animals or small children," Winnie offered hopefully. "And I spend a good part of every day in my old rocker."

"Can you have a cat in your condo?"

"I can."

"Can what?" Randolph asked as he joined us on the porch. I think he wanted to be sure I was going to leave with the dog.

"Have a cat," Winnie said.

At first I thought her son was going to protest the idea, but then he smiled. "A cat would be a perfect solution, but when I suggested it, you said that a cat could never replace Bella."

"I did say that," Winnie admitted, "but that was before I knew there was a cat that needed a human just like me. Can I meet her?" Winnie asked me.

I glanced at Randolph. He nodded his head in the affirmative.

"I'll go and get her. If you like her, you can take her on a trial basis. If it works out, we'll do the adoption paperwork later."

"We're leaving in two hours," Randolph warned me.

"I'll be back in less than one. I'll donate a cat carrier, a litter box, litter, and food so you can get her settled when you get to your new place. I even have some of the special salmon treats she loves. It may take her a few days to adjust to her new situation, but I think the two of you will be perfect together."

Winnie was actually smiling as I loaded Bella in the truck, and I felt a whole lot better about taking her than I had when I'd first arrived.

Bella and Charlie got along fabulously, so I decided to leave them at the boathouse while I went to visit my parents. I called Ellie and told her about the newest member of our family, in case she arrived at the boathouse before I did. My parents greeted me at the door of their new home, handed me a glass of wine, and told me they had something important to discuss with me. My heart sank as they led me to the deck and asked me to take a seat. Ever since my mom came back to town and I found out I was going to be a sister, I've held a secret fear that eventually Mom would leave—she always does—and take Harper with her.

"Thanks for coming by," Mom said nervously. "Your dad and I have something important to discuss with you."

"Please don't leave," I begged.

"What?" Mom looked surprised. "I'm not leaving."

I let out a long breath. "You aren't?"

"Of course not." Mom sat down next to me and took my hand. "Your dad and I are getting married, and I want you to be my maid of honor."

"Married! You're getting married?" I jumped up and grabbed my mom in an extremely exuberant hug.

"Oh my God I am so happy," I cried.

"Don't I get a hug?" Dad asked.

I let Mom go long enough to hug my dad and then pulled them both into my arms.

"When?"

"Right away," Mom answered. "We don't want a big ceremony. Just you and Harper and Pappy."

"And Zak, of course," Dad added.

"Are you sure? We can do something nice at Zak's. It doesn't have to be huge, but you could invite a few friends and have a reception."

"It seems a little silly to go to all that trouble at this point," Mom said. "We have two children together."

"Maybe, but it's the first and only wedding for both of you," I pointed out. "Please think about it. I'll do everything. All you'll have to do is show up."

Mom hesitated and looked at Dad.

"We'd need to keep it small," Dad insisted.

"You can make up the guest list," I assured him.

"And I don't think I want to bother with the whole white dress thing," Mom added.

"We can do a theme. It will be fun and less formal," I suggested.

"A theme?" Mom asked.

"Yeah." I shrugged. "Like Hawaiian or nautical. We could all wear veils and do Arabian Nights."

"I'm not wearing a veil," Dad said.

"Can your dad and I have a couple of days to talk about it?" Mom asked.

"Of course. It *is* your wedding. I'm just so thrilled you guys are finally getting hitched that I'll be happy with whatever you decide."

I picked up Harper, who was propped up in her infant seat.

"Did you hear?" I held her in my arms and looked into her bright blue eyes. "We're going to have a daddy *and* a mommy."

Harper smiled.

"Oh, I have to show you the outfits I got for her." I adjusted my baby sis so that she was resting on my shoulder, then returned to the house for the bag of goodies I'd brought back from my trip.

"I got a bunch of things, but this is my favorite."

I held up a tiny lace dress in a pale yellow with a matching hat that looked like something one would wear to a garden party.

"Adorable." Mom took it from me. "Maybe we should do afternoon garden party for our theme. The women could wear sundresses and floppy hats and the men could wear casual dress attire."

"I love it," I said. And I did.

"Zak's deck and pool area is already pretty awesome, but we could add huge bouquets of flowers in a variety of bright and summery colors. I'm sure Hazel will help with the arrangements. She's really into her flowers, and since she's dating Pappy, we'll have to invite her anyway. I can ask Ellie to cater the food, and I'm sure Levi will help set up. Jeremy can do the music."

"Doesn't Jeremy belong to a heavy metal band?" Dad asked.

"Yeah, but he can play all types of music. Give him a list of what you want and I'm sure he can do it. This is going to be so awesome."

"And small," Dad reminded me.

"Of course," I agreed.

"If we're going to actually *have* a wedding, I'll need to invite my parents and a few other members of my family," Mom pointed out.

"I'm sure that won't be a problem," I said. I looked at Dad, who was frowning. "We'll just invite family and a few friends," I assured him.

By the time the big day rolled around, I would look back to this moment and realize how foolish I was to think that small was even a possibility.

"I've joined a dating site," Ellie informed me after I'd returned to the boathouse to meet her for dinner. Both Charlie and Bella greeted me as I walked through the door as if I'd been away for days rather than a couple of hours. I gave them both welcoming hugs before answering.

"Dating site? Like online dating?"

"Basically." Ellie followed me across the room as I headed to the back door to let the dogs out for a run on the beach. "You register and fill out a profile. After you do that, you're given a list of men who seem to meet your requirements. Some of them live too far away to actually date, but others live in the general area."

"When did you do this?" I wondered as I stepped outside to make sure Bella wouldn't run off. I knew she was a well-behaved dog, but she'd only been with me for a short time, so I wasn't certain how she'd react to being off leash without being in a fenced yard. "We just got home yesterday."

"I filled out the profile last night and I've already found a man."

"Wow. That was fast."

I had to hand it to Ellie. Once she set her mind to something, she made it happen.

"I really lucked out and found someone who lives just down the mountain in Bryton Lake. He's perfect." Ellie beamed as she began scooping servings of the buffalo chicken casserole she'd brought onto ceramic plates after the dogs had returned to the boathouse and were having their own dinner.

"Perfect how?" I asked as I poured two glasses of wine and set them on the small dining table that was tucked into the corner of my main living space. I love my boathouse, but it really is tiny.

"He's a thirty-four-year-old business owner who travels a lot but definitely wants a house and children to come home to." Ellie added bread from the oven to the plates. "We IM'd back and forth for hours and he seems really nice."

"Are you planning to go on an actual date?" I asked as I took a sip of the best wine I'd ever tasted.

Ellie hesitated. "We are. Hopefully this week. Maybe even tomorrow. It's just that . . ."

"Just that what?" I asked.

"Just that Kevin has a friend in town, and the only way he can get away this week is if I bring a friend to even things out. I was hoping you'd come along."

"You want me to go on a double date with you?" I asked as Ellie placed our plates on the table next to the silverware I'd already set out.

"Not a date exactly. I mean, you don't have to actually do anything with this guy. I just need someone to round out the party."

"I have a boyfriend," I reminded Ellie as I took a bite of the delicious casserole.

"I know, but it's just for one night."

"Tabasco sauce?" I asked.

Ellie frowned at my response.

"The casserole. Is that Tabasco sauce that gives the chicken that kick?"

"Buffalo sauce," she confirmed. "So back to the date. I really need you to come."

I knew that I absolutely should say no. I was practically engaged.

"Please," she added.

I took a sip of my wine and considered the request. The food was delicious, but Ellie hadn't eaten a thing. I could see that she was really focused on this date, which wasn't like her at all. I supposed that getting back on the horse was her way of dealing with the heartache Rob had left her.

"Where are you going?" I finally asked.

"The Wharf," Ellie said, referring to an upscale restaurant in town.

"I'll have to run this crazy idea past Zak," I warned her.

"You can call him now."

I frowned.

"Please. This guy is perfect. I really want a chance to meet him before he meets someone else."

"If he's perfect, don't you think he'll wait?"

Ellie just looked at me with giant brown eyes. I knew she'd had it tough lately and could really use a new man in her life.

"Okay, I'll call Zak."

"Thank you, thank you." Ellie hugged me.

I took out my phone and dialed Zak's cell. This would be an interesting conversation.

I got his voice mail.

"Hey, Zak. I was wondering if you cared if I went out on a date tomorrow night. Call me back when you get this message."

I'd barely hung up when my phone rang.

"You want to go on a date?" Zak asked. I'd left him two other messages today that he hadn't returned, but I guess I just hadn't given him the right incentive.

"Where are you?" I asked. The sound of video games was clear in the background.

"A video arcade with Scooter. I was going to call you back when we finished up in here, but when I got your message . . ."

I laughed.

"I thought we were okay." Zak had to shout to be heard over the sound of bells and whistles.

"We are," I assured him. "Finish your game and call me from outside. I can barely hear you."

"Five minutes," Zak insisted. "I'll call you in five minutes."

"Okay."

I hung up.

"I think I may have given Zak a heart attack."

"I should think so," Ellie responded as she dug into her food. I guess her appetite had returned once I agreed to her crazy plan. "Why didn't you explain the whole thing in the message?"

"I guess I figured we could discuss the details when he called back. I didn't know he was in an arcade and couldn't hear anything. He's going to call back in five minutes."

"You are a mean woman, Zoe Donovan."

"Hey, you're the one who's insisting I cheat on my boyfriend," I pointed out.

"I'm not asking you to cheat. I just need you to go on a date. It's totally different," Ellie insisted.

I laughed.

My phone rang. It was Zak.

"That was only two minutes," I said.

"I hurried," Zak explained. "So about this date . . ."

"Don't have a coronary. It's not a real date," I assured him. I filled him in on the details.

"So you called and gave me a heart attack so you could ask me if I minded if you went on a double date with Ellie so she can hook up with a man she's never met?" Zak clarified.

"Yup."

Zak paused. I suppose it was only fair to give him a minute to process things.

"Can I meet him first?" Zak asked.

"The date is tomorrow and you're in Kansas," I pointed out.

"Yeah, about that." Zak hesitated. "I'm flying home in the morning."

I knew that Zak had planned to spend at least a week. Maybe two. Things must not be going well. "That wasn't a very long visit. Isn't Scooter disappointed?"

"No." Zak sounded like he was hiding something. "Scooter is coming with me."

"You're babysitting again?"

"Sort of. Scooter is bored, and I worked it out with his father for him to come to visit me for a while."

"I see. How long?"

I like Scooter okay, but he *is* a handful, and between my parents' wedding and going on dates with Ellie, my free time was going to be pretty limited as it was.

"Six weeks," Zak answered.

I might have momentarily blacked out at that point.

"Zoe? Are you still there?"

"Yeah." I groaned. "I'm here."

"I know it's a long visit, and I know we have things to work out between us, but poor Scooter really needs a friend."

I took a deep breath. "I know. And I love you for being so concerned about him."

"So it's okay?"

"We aren't married or even living together. You don't have to ask my permission if you want to have a friend sleep over," I teased. "Did you forget that you have a new dog to break in as well?"

"Bella and Scooter will love each other," Zak assured me. "Did things go okay when you picked her up?"

"It was tough at first, but then I remembered Sheba."

"Sheba?"

"That longhaired black cat I've been trying to find a quiet home for. Winnie was going to take her for a trial run, but when the two met, it was love at first sight. I think they'll be very happy together."

"That's good. So about this date . . ." Zak returned to the original subject.

"I'll have him pick me up at your house so he can meet my boyfriend."

Chapter 4

Wednesday, July 9

I'd arranged to meet Pandora and Boomer at Ellie's Beach Hut for lunch. I hoped they'd accept the decision of the committee and we could all share a relaxing lunch. Of course, even though this was my hope, my *expectation* was that all hell would break loose as the pair debated the merits of each approach to the contest. I knew that Ellie's would be packed on an afternoon in July, so I called ahead and asked her to reserve us a table.

Situated on the pier of one of the most popular beaches at the lake, the eatery had been plagued with long lines since Memorial Day. I knew that Ellie had applied to the county planning department for the right to add additional seating on the outdoor deck during the busiest summer months, although I questioned whether her tiny kitchen could accommodate a larger crowd even if her application was approved. Ellie did utilize outdoor grills during the summer, so with an additional employee or two, her plan could pan out.

When I arrived at Ellie's, Boomer and Pandora were already seated at a premium table along the railing that separated the pier from the water. From a distance, they appeared to be chatting agreeably. I let myself relax. Just a little. We were able to make our greetings and order our food before the real fireworks began.

Pandora Parker is a unique individual. She's a tiny thing barely tipping the height charts at five foot one. In spite of the fact that she's known for her tendency to be *very* outspoken, she's a hit with the male members of the classic car circuit due primarily, I suspect, to long blond hair that brushes her waist when left to its own devices and bright blue eyes framed by impossibly long, thick eyelashes.

After we ordered, I explained to Pandora and Boomer the committee's decision to continue with a coed event.

"The fact that a bunch of pansies tend to enter this tournament shouldn't prevent those of us with the balls to actually take out our opponent from competing," Pandora argued as she polished off a huge burger with a double patty and a truckload of fries even I couldn't finish.

"It's that attitude that has the guys so pissed off," pointed out Boomer, who was tall and dark, with broad shoulders and a boyish grin. "We both know that you winning the tournament last year was a fluke. The guys simply aren't comfortable ramming into an itty-bitty thing like you. After everything was done, the opinion among the men was that everyone tried to avoid you because they were afraid that one good jolt would kill you."

"Like hell." Pandora's long braid almost hit Boomer in the face as she whipped her head around to look him directly in the eye. "I won because I'm the best driver, and those panty wipes you call friends are suffering the aftereffects of a bruised ego. The committee voted to let us compete against one another, and the divas and I intend to do just that."

"Well, the guys and I are going to appeal the committee decision," Boomer shot back.

I decided to tune out while Pandora and Boomer duked it out. The headache I'd had when I arrived had turned into a migraine two minutes after I'd sat down with the pair. Both were really exceptional people, but once they got going, who knew how long they would maintain their debate. In addition to being genetically gifted, they were bright and focused, which made them natural leaders in their field. I knew that each realized they were arguing not only for themselves but for the unofficial team of drivers they represented.

Five other women had entered the event, the front-runner among them besides Pandora being Jugs, nicknamed for the surgically enhanced body feature of the same name. I knew she had competed in derbies in other towns and had done quite well. Jugs and Pandora were friends and had been traveling to events together for as long as I'd known them.

In addition to Pandora and Jugs, the four others were Zelda, a tall woman with broad shoulders and a deep voice who towered over most of the men; Jaqui, an exotic-looking woman who carried a knife on her thigh and, I suspected, had at one time belonged to a street gang; Rizo, a ditzy blonde with a charming sense of humor but little going on intellectually; and Pepper, a quiet little thing who worked for Pandora and followed her around like a dutiful puppy.

The seven men led by Boomer, who was clearly the favorite to win the event, had all competed in the tournament before: Masher, a giant of a man, and probably the only one who could take down Zelda in a wrestling match; Crusher, a boyish blond who took a disturbing amount of glee in destroying things; the Pencil Triplets, so named due to their tall, pencil-thin frames; and Big Boy Branson, who was known for being as wide as he was tall.

There were three men new to the competition this year: Dezee, a quiet man who was small in stature and had a tendency to drift off while you were talking to him; Bruiser, a tiny man with a big ego I doubted he'd be able to live up to; and a boy-child with an outrageous personality who went by the name of Crank.

"Okay, so we're agreed," Pandora exclaimed as she shook hands with Boomer.

Uh-oh.

"Agreed to what?" I asked.

"Boomer and I are going to compete in a road race at sunrise. The winner gets to decide if we have a coed or segregated tournament."

"Road race?" I paled. This was not going to go over well.

"We'll start at just beyond the town limit and race to the summit," Boomer decided.

"You know, there's a huge curve at the top of the summit," I pointed out. "It's really tight. In fact, we refer to it as dead man's curve."

"Sounds perfect," Pandora agreed.

"Salinger will never allow this," I tried.

"So we won't tell him," Pandora said.

"I'm not sure that the committee is going to go along with this," I tried. "We did vote after all, and a decision has been made."

Pandora looked at Boomer. "How about it? Are you comfortable with allowing the committee to make such an important decision?"

"You know," Boomer grinned, "I can't say that I am."

"Yeah," Pandora agreed. "Me neither. It's our derby, so I say we decide."

"Actually it's the town's derby," I pointed out.

"Wouldn't be much of a derby if we all pulled out," Pandora threatened.

"Okay, I guess I see your point, but maybe we should consider flipping a coin or choosing a number between one and ten."

"I'm not going to let a coin toss decide something so important," Pandora insisted. "Chances are what we decide this year will set a precedent for the future."

"Yeah, but a road race sounds dangerous, and I'm pretty sure it isn't legal," I tried again.

"Pandora and I are professional drivers. We've participated in drag races all over the country. The race won't be a problem, and if we do it early, Salinger will never know."

"But there could be other traffic."

"Which you can manage if you get there early. Bring some of those orange cones to close off the road."

I did have orange cones, but I still wasn't sure this was the best idea. I could see that Boomer and Pandora had made up their minds, however, so I supposed it was best that I showed up to keep an eye on things.

"What time are we talking?" I asked.

"Sunrise is at 5:40. We'll line up at mile marker twenty-four at 5:30. Zoe can be the judge as long as she's going to be there. Do you have someone you can bring to help out at the starting line?"

"Five-thirty?" I groaned.

"We need a judge," Pandora pointed out.

"Okay," I agreed. "Five-thirty. I'll see if I can talk Levi into coming."

"Excellent." Pandora grinned. "I've been wanting to spend some time with your cute friend."

"Better start reworking those groups." Boomer smiled confidently. "I guess this is going to be a segregated event after all."

"Save your time; I've got this in the bag." Pandora stood up and sauntered out the door.

I had my eye on Boomer as he watched her leave. For the first time since I'd sat down with this gristly pair, I noticed something that hadn't previously occurred to me. Pandora and Boomer were totally in to each other. As odd as it may sound, I really think all this volleying back and forth is some sort of really disturbing foreplay. I thought about my early relationship with Zak. All the verbal banter really had been the result of a deeply felt attraction. Maybe this tournament would be more interesting than I had originally thought.

Chapter 5

Thursday, July 10

I don't know what I was thinking, agreeing to meet Boomer and Pandora at 5:30 in the morning. Not only was it much too early to be out of my nice warm bed but it was much too cold to be wandering around on the summit. Summer in the mountains is not like summer in the valley, where the nighttime temperatures rival the daytime ones. Most summer days see a forty-degree swing between the high temperature and the low. If I had to guess, I'd say the current temperature was hovering around forty degrees.

I snuggled into my sweatshirt and stifled a yawn. I really should have thought to bring a thermos of coffee with me rather than just a travel mug. The last twenty-four hours had been *really* hectic. Not only had Zak arrived with Scooter yesterday afternoon, creating quite a bit of chaos, but I'd had my big double date with Ellie as well. I took a long sip of my coffee and waited for Pandora to arrive. It was 5:35 and she'd yet to make an appearance.

"Looks like we're all dressed up for a party, but the guest of honor is a no-show," Levi commented as he walked up behind me, sipping from his own travel mug filled with liquid adrenaline.

"I'm sure she'll be here."

Actually, I wasn't, but I didn't want to admit quite yet that I'd dragged Levi out so early for nothing.

"So how was the big date last night?" Levi teased. "Did everything go as hoped?"

I rolled my eyes. "To be honest, I figured that once I told the guy he needed to pick me up at my boyfriend's house, he'd think I was nuts and I wouldn't have to go on the date. But he didn't flinch."

"So he was nice?"

I wrapped my arms around my waist and turned my back to the wind that was whipping over the mountain. It felt more like January than July.

"No, he was crazy. And sort of creepy," I added as I pulled my hood over my head. "In fact, I wouldn't be surprised if that wasn't the first time he'd picked up a date at her boyfriend's."

Levi laughed. "And Ellie's date?"

"A swing and a miss."

"Poor Ellie." Levi grinned.

I'd noticed immediately that he didn't look all that broken up about Ellie's lousy date. If I know Levi, and I do, I'm willing to bet that, although he isn't ready to make the type of commitment to Ellie that she needs, he doesn't want anyone else making a commitment to her either.

"He might not have been *the one*, but Ellie's not giving up," I cautioned him. "She has another date tonight, and thankfully, I haven't been asked to go along."

"She's really serious about this baby thing?"

"She is," I confirmed. "She seems determined to have her own little bundle of joy by this time next year, one way or another. I just hope she's not setting herself up for more heartache. She's trying so hard to find the perfect man that I think she's unintentionally sabotaging the whole thing."

"What do you mean?" Levi asked.

I cupped my hands together and blew into them in an attempt to warm them up. "Ellie and this guy Kevin seemed to hit it off at first. I didn't get a good vibe from him, but Ellie really seemed to like him, so I thought they might make a connection. Problem was that two minutes after we'd ordered our meal, Ellie was quizzing him about his stance on children. She wanted to know how soon he wanted them and how many he saw himself having. Don't get me wrong: the guy was pretty odd and I'm not unhappy about the fact that Ellie scared him off, but in my opinion even if she finds Mr. Right, he's never going to stick around long enough to find out if they can make a go of it."

"Maybe that's for the best," Levi stated. "Ellie doesn't need to get involved with some random guy she meets on the Internet. She needs . . ." Levi hesitated.

I knew he was going to say *me* but stopped himself at the last minute.

"Unless you've changed your mind about a houseful of offspring, you need to move on and let Ellie do the same. She's never going to be happy in a relationship that doesn't include children."

"Yeah, I know." Levi sighed. "She's only twenty-five. I don't get the hurry."

"Ellie has always had a maternal streak. Remember when we were in high school and she used to bail on us anytime she managed to line up a babysitting gig? And it wasn't about the money. Ellie really loves kids, and spending time with Hannah gave her a taste of what it would be like to have her own child."

"Maybe she can just get back into babysitting," Levi suggested.

"I think she's way past that."

Levi didn't say anything. He knew I was right, even if he didn't want to admit it.

We both diverted our attention to the spectators who had gathered to watch the race. Pandora really *should* have been here by now.

"Looks like the natives are getting restless," Levi observed as people in the crowd were beginning to grumble.

"If she isn't here in five minutes, she forfeits and we win," a large man with a deep voice who I recognized as Boomer's friend Masher declared.

"She'll be here," Jugs responded.

I could tell by her expression that Jugs was less confident than she was trying to appear. It did seem odd that Pandora would be late to the event after her display of confidence the previous afternoon. In addition to Jugs, two other divas had shown up for the race, while Boomer had been accompanied by three other men.

I was disappointed the men and women wouldn't be competing together in the derby, but I hadn't been a fan of the race idea in the first place, so maybe it was just as well that Pandora was late. I was preparing to call it a forfeit when Pandora's street car, which was the exact same light pink shade as her derby car, rolled up.

"Okay, let's do this thing," Jugs shouted as Pandora revved her engine.

Talk about making an entrance. Pandora hadn't even gotten out of the car. She'd come prepared to race dressed in her signature pink racing suit and pink helmet and pulled right up to the starting line. Boomer pulled on his helmet and jumped into his tricked-out Mustang. Jugs, Boomer, Zelda, and I were instructed to make our way down to the finish line, while the other representatives from both the men's and women's groups stayed at the starting line with Levi to ensure a fair start. I have to admit that my pulse was racing with anticipation at the race that would be concluded within seconds. There was something about the smell of exhaust and the roar of the engines that sent my nerve endings into hyperdrive.

The whole exciting, terrifying, tragic event took less time than it would take me to retell the story. The cars shot from the starting point, bumper to bumper until Pandora pulled away at the last second. The crowd roared with cheers of victory until the moment we realized that Pandora hadn't stopped after crossing the finish line but had continued on toward the sharp curve and the rocky cliff that plummeted a quarter mile to the valley below. I held my breath as Pandora skidded into the curve, appearing to make the adjustment needed to make the turn at the last minute. As she slid around the bend, it looked like she had all but stopped. I had just released my breath when I heard the sound of an explosion after the car plunged over the side and burst into flames upon impact with the valley floor.

"Oh my God," I screamed as I ran toward the place where the car had knocked out the barrier. I can't say I remember exactly what happened after that. Flames shot into the air as everyone screamed and cried while Levi, Boomer, and a couple of his guys, tried to make their way down the steep embankment. I vaguely remember calling 911. The sound of sirens and the image of flashing lights as rescue workers arrived at the scene still resides in a corner of my mind. And I don't think I'll ever forget the smell of fuel as the fire department showed up to try to contain the blaze.

Willa called an emergency meeting of the events committee. We had thousands of people preparing to ascend to our little town for the classic car show and demolition derby and no one knew if we should continue with the event or not.

"We've spoken to the more than one hundred men and women who have entered their cars in the show and all have agreed that the show should go on," Willa announced. "The only event scheduled for today is the classic car parade. It will be held as planned. We're waiting to make a decision as to whether we should continue with the derby. The qualifying rounds are scheduled for tomorrow. We're in the process of interviewing all of the participants. Boomer is definitely out, but most of the others seem willing to compete. We still need to track down Pepper and Dezee."

"Neither Pepper nor Dezee were at the race," I informed the group.

"I did think it odd that Pepper hadn't been there," Levi shared. "Pepper was closer to Pandora than anyone. You'd think she'd come out for the big race."

Not only did Pepper work for Pandora as a bookkeeper for her repair shop but she traveled with her to all of the car shows she participated in as well. The pair seemed to have forged a strong friendship over the years.

"Perhaps Pepper and Dezee stayed behind to keep an eye on the cars," Dad suggested.

It was common practice for each team to assign someone to watch the cars when they weren't being used. As unfortunate as it may seem, tampering to rig races and other events was not as uncommon as one would like to believe.

"I'm sure they'll show up," Hazel said.

"Either way, it would be great if you could let me know whether the derby is a go or not as soon as you come to a decision," I told them. If the derby was going to take place with at least two fewer drivers, I was going to need to rework the groups.

"Has anyone heard what happened?" Levi asked. "Salinger was pretty closemouthed at the scene. Pandora was a more than competent driver, but it looked like she simply lost control of her car."

"We don't have any news yet, I'm afraid," Willa verified. "I'm sure Sheriff Salinger will fill us in once he knows anything."

"I feel like this is all my fault," I confided to Levi after Willa adjourned the meeting.

"Your fault? How can it be your fault?"

"I should have done more to stop them and I didn't."

"Boomer and Pandora are adults and therefore responsible for their own decisions," Levi pointed out. "From what you told me, you did try to warn them of the inherent danger, and they chose to race anyway. They're professional drivers who know what they're doing."

"Pandora is dead," I said.

"That's true." Levi sighed. "I know you feel bad and I do too, but I honestly don't know what you could have done to stop them."

"I could have told Salinger."

"Maybe. And maybe if you had, Pandora would be alive, but what would more likely have occurred is that Salinger would have blown you off like he always does."

"Yeah, maybe."

"I know you feel responsible, but don't beat yourself up over this," Levi counseled. "There's nothing you can do at this point to change the outcome of this very tragic event."

After Levi left, I called Zak, who informed me that he'd taken Scooter, Bella, and Charlie to the beach. They'd packed a picnic and planned to make a day of it. I really wanted to talk to Zak about my feelings about the race, but I didn't think the timing was quite right and I didn't want to ruin his day with Scooter.

I then called Jeremy, who assured me that he had everything under control if I wanted to take the day off after the harrowing experience.

I considered my options. On one hand, it would be fun to join Zak, Scooter, and the dogs at the beach. Zak and I had had virtually no time together since the awkward moment when he proposed and I froze, and I felt that it was necessary to our future relationship to clear the air. Zak had assured me that we were fine and that he understood my hesitation, but honestly, I was less than certain that *fine* defined his true feelings on the subject.

Of course, Zak and I wouldn't really be able to talk. Scooter was *very* excited about spending the summer with Zak, and his tendency to operate in hyperdrive had been obvious from the moment I'd picked them up at the airport yesterday. I hoped that after a day or two he'd settle in and settle down.

Luckily, Bella seemed to love the active little boy, so my fear that we'd have another dog-bite incident to deal with where Scooter was concerned had been nicely laid to rest.

I'd never had breakfast, so I considered stopping by Ellie's for a bite to eat, but first, I decided, I was going to head over to the Ashton Falls Motor Inn to see if I could find out where Pepper and Dezee had gotten off to. Until I had their decision regarding the derby, I really wouldn't be able to rework the groups, which was something I needed to do by the end of the day.

I knocked on the door of the motel room Pepper and Pandora had been sharing, but there was no answer. I tried the handle and the door opened easily. I hate to admit it, but when I walked into the room, I screamed like a girl. This is a confession I am not proud of. I'm one of those people who roll my eyes when some girl on television stumbles upon a dead body and starts screaming uncontrollably. I mean, really, who does that? I might gasp if startled, but screaming on and on and on and on? Well, you get the picture.

Anyway, I walked through the door and screamed, not because I'd seen a dead body but because I'd seen a live one.

"Pandora?"

"What time is it?" a very much alive derby diva asked. She had been sleeping when I'd come in.

"You're dead," I accused her.

"I'm not dead. Maybe a little hung over, but certainly not dead."

"But you are," I insisted. "I saw you die."

Pandora looked at me like I'd lost my mind.

"You raced Boomer this morning. I saw you. You lost control and went over the embankment. Your car exploded. I'm certain of that."

"I missed the race," Pandora insisted. "Have you been smoking the funny cigarettes that were passed around last night?"

"No." I took a deep breath and tried to gather my thoughts. If Pandora was alive, who was dead?

"When was the last time you saw Pepper?" I asked.

Pandora squinted against the massive headache I suspected she was fighting. "We partied together last night. I got really drunk, which is odd because it usually takes a lot to get me drunk. Dezee walked me back here and Pepper put me to bed. That's the last thing I remember." Pandora looked at the bedside clock. "I guess I must have forfeited the race."

"No," I informed her. "You won."

"I did? I must have been drunker than I thought. I don't even remember racing."

"I don't think you did."

"Huh?"

"Back to Pepper. Did you see her this morning?"

Pandora squinted. I could tell that her head must be pounding. "I'm not sure. Why?"

"She's missing. I think she may be dead."

"Dead? What are you saying?" Pandora jumped out of the bed totally naked.

"Someone showed up for the race this morning in your car. The person who raced won and then died. Everyone thinks it was you, but here you are. No one has seen Pepper."

"Oh God." Pandora bent over and vomited into the wastebasket.

"Perhaps you should get dressed," I suggested.

Pandora pulled on a pair of shorts and a halter. She didn't seem to care about undergarments, but to each her own.

"Tell me exactly what happened." Pandora sat down on the bed next to me.

I explained the series of events that led me to this place and time.

"She must have decided to race for me." Pandora began to cry.

"What happened last night?" I asked.

Pandora stared off into space like I wasn't even in the room. I supposed she really cared about Pepper and was having a hard time accepting what I was telling her.

"Honestly, I don't know. Boomer and some of the guys invited me and some of the girls to party in his room. Pepper hadn't wanted to go. She thought I should have an early night so that I'd be ready for the race, but I was bored and antsy and didn't see how a couple of drinks could hurt. After a bit of negotiation, she agreed to go along with me, but then she took off shortly after we arrived. I was having fun and didn't want to leave, so I told her that I was going to stay and have a couple more."

"But you had more than a couple," I deducted.

"But I didn't. I don't know what happened. I can usually put away more alcohol than Masher, and that's saying a lot. Oh God," Pandora sobbed. "I can't believe Pepper is dead."

"I don't *know* at this point that the dead woman is Pepper," I offered. "I guess we should call Salinger."

Pandora looked at me with empty eyes.

Chapter 6

Pandora had been talking with Salinger in his office for hours. I'm not sure why I waited dutifully in the reception area. It wasn't like I could do anything to help Pandora through the terror of knowing that her best friend had died trying to fulfill the commitment she was too hung over to deal with herself. I tried to imagine how I'd feel if something happened to Ellie or Levi due to my negligence, but the terror the mere thought brought about was much more than I could handle.

I called Jeremy and told him that I wouldn't be in at all that day and then Willa, to give her an update on the situation. Once I'd informed Salinger of Pandora's undead state of being, he'd called the coroner to take a closer look at what was left of the body, which had been burned beyond recognition.

I also spoke with Zak, briefly telling him about the major twist in the events of the day. He'd offered to come down to the station and sit with me, but there wasn't really anything he could do, and I didn't want to interrupt his day with Scooter. I guess Zak must have called Levi after we hung up because he showed up with a take-out bag containing a sandwich and fries from Ellie's.

"You really didn't have to come down here," I said as I gratefully accepted the food.

"Of course I needed to come. You should have called me right away," Levi scolded.

"I know. It's just been a really long couple of days and I'm feeling a bit overwhelmed."

"Zak wanted to come down, but with it being Scooter's first day in Ashton Falls, he hated to leave the boy alone with some random babysitter," Levi informed me.

"Yeah, I get it. I told him not to interrupt his day at the lake."

"You should call him later, or better yet stop by. I could tell he was feeling very conflicted and just a bit frantic that he couldn't be here for you."

"Has Zak said anything to you," I lowered my voice, even though the receptionist had wandered off and there was no one else in the room, "about the engagement fiasco?"

"Not really. Guys don't yammer on about things like that the way you women do."

"He didn't say anything at all?" I prodded.

"Like what?" Levi actually looked confused.

"I don't know. It's just that I haven't had a chance to really *talk* to Zak about the whole thing. He says we're fine, but I guess I have my doubts."

"So ask him," Levi suggested.

"I was going to, but at first I didn't know what to say, and then he sat with you on the flight home from Hawaii so I didn't get a chance to talk to him, and then he immediately headed to Kansas to visit with Scooter. I picked him up at the airport yesterday, but Scooter was with him so we couldn't talk."

"So talk to him tonight after Scooter goes to bed. Zak really hasn't said anything, but I know he loves you. I'm sure it's fine."

"Ellie thinks I made a huge mistake."

Levi paused. I imagine he was considering whether *he* believed I'd made a huge mistake.

"Zak loves you and I know you love him, but I don't think you made a mistake. Just because you care deeply for someone doesn't mean you're ready to make some huge, life-altering decision."

"But Ellie said—" I began.

"We talked about that this morning. Ellie wants to get married and have a family, so she can't understand why everyone else doesn't feel the same way," Levi interrupted. "I don't think marriage is something you should jump into if you aren't ready."

"But how do you know when you *are* ready?"

Levi shrugged. "I guess you just do."

"Zak is ready and we're the same age. I love him so much. I can't imagine my life without him. I really don't know why I hesitated."

"Zak is different from you and me." Levi put his arm around me. "His timetable and your timetable might not be the same, but that doesn't mean one is better than the other."

"Different how?" I asked.

"When we were in high school, we spent our free time going to parties, hanging out at the beach, and hooking up with our crush of the moment, while Zak was building a software empire in his garage. You and I are just coming into our adulthood, but Zak— and, to some degree, Ellie—have been living the adult lifestyle for quite some time."

Levi had a point. Zak was already a mature and highly respected businessman while I was partying my way through my early twenties.

"So what do I do to catch up?" I wondered.

"Nothing. You're perfect the way you are. You'll find your own way in your own time, and my guess is that Zak will wait for you."

I smiled. I really did feel better. "Thanks, Levi." I hugged him.

"Salinger sure is taking his own sweet time," Levi observed.

"I suppose he just wants to be sure he gets everything out of Pandora that he can before she sobers up and decides not to cooperate."

"Why wouldn't she cooperate?" Levi asked.

I shrugged. "I don't know. I just have a weird feeling about this whole thing. It looks like the body in the car most likely belonged to Pepper. Pandora must feel guilty. Sometimes feeling guilty can make you defensive."

"Yeah, I guess I can see that. Poor Pepper. What was she doing driving Pandora's car in the first place?"

"We don't know. Pandora is *really* hung over. I suspect that Pepper tried to wake her this morning and, when she was unsuccessful, decided to show up at the race in Pandora's place."

"I've partied with Pandora," Levi informed me. "She can drink more than guys twice her size. But it doesn't seem like her to drink so much before a big race."

"She said she only had a couple," I explained as I dug into my lunch.

Levi frowned. "That makes no sense at all."

"I've been thinking about it. What if Pandora was drugged?"

"Drugged? Who would drug her?" Levi wondered.

"Maybe one of the guys was trying to force her to forfeit. Maybe they figured that Boomer wasn't going to win against a very determined little diva and decided that taking her out of the running was the best way to go. I know Pandora has managed to bruise quite a few male egos as of late."

"I don't know. Boomer talks the talk, but I can tell he cares about Pandora. In fact, I think he more than cares about her. I really don't see him drugging her."

"Maybe it wasn't Boomer. Pandora said that Boomer invited her to hang out in his room, but several of the others were there as well. I think I'm going to suggest that Salinger do a drug test on Pandora if she'll agree. It might tell us how an experienced drinker got so slammed on a couple of drinks."

I wondered if they'd ever found Dezee. I knew that Pepper and Dezee had been friends prior to his entering the competition this year. I wasn't sure exactly how they knew each other, but when I'd mentioned to Jugs this morning that I found it odd that Pepper wasn't there, she'd commented that she might have spent the night with Dezee. She didn't know for a fact that they were a couple, but she suspected as much because she knew that the reason Dezee bought a car and entered the competition in the first place was so he could travel around the country with Pepper and Pandora.

I tried to figure out who else wasn't present for the race that morning.

I remembered seeing Zelda but not Jaqui or Rizo, and while Boomer, Masher, Big Boy Branson, Bruiser, and two of the Pencil Triplets had shown up, the third Triplet, Crank, and Crusher were all missing.

It was feasible that all those who didn't attend were either guarding the cars for their team or nursing their own hangovers, but I decided that when it came to creating a list of suspects responsible for drugging Pandora—if she was indeed drugged—the missing entrants in the derby competition would be a good place to start.

"I wish they'd hurry up. This waiting around is stressful," Levi complained.

"If you think this is stressful for us, just think of what Pandora must be going through. I'm afraid this whole thing is going to destroy her. She was really upset when she realized what had happened."

"Here she comes," Levi said as we watched Pandora walking down the hall from Salinger's office.

"You waited." Pandora seemed surprised to see Levi and me sitting in the lobby.

"We wanted to be here for you," I offered.

Pandora looked confused.

"To help. If you need help."

"What kind of help?"

It was evident that Pandora wasn't used to people being around to support her during hard times.

"I don't know. Like give you a ride. Provide a sounding board if you need to rant. A shoulder if you need to cry."

Pandora smiled. "Thanks. That's nice."

"Are you hungry?" Levi asked.

Again Pandora looked confused. I assumed that she was still suffering from the aftershock of everything that had happened.

"We can get a bite to eat. Maybe talk," he offered.

"Okay."

It didn't seem that Pandora cared one way or the other, but Levi gently took her hand and led her out to his car. I had my own truck, so we agreed to meet at the Beach Hut. I had my phone out to call ahead and have Ellie save us a table when an incoming call from Salinger showed up on my screen.

"Hey, Salinger. What's up?"

I know the two of us butt heads from time to time, but we're actually becoming friends after working together on so many different investigations.

"I hoped to catch you before you left. I have a few questions for you, if you don't mind."

"I don't mind." I had already eaten, after all. "I'll call Levi and let him know what I'd doing and then come back inside. I'm still on the walkway in front of the building."

After calling Levi and explaining what was going on, I called Ellie and gave her a heads-up that Levi was on his way over with Pandora and then headed back in through the double front doors and down the hall to Salinger's office, which I have become *very* familiar with. I'm not entirely sure where the woman who runs the front desk had gone off to, but she'd disappeared shortly after I arrived and was still missing.

"Have a seat." Salinger pointed to one of the hard plastic chairs that were placed on the opposite side of the desk from where he sat. "I wanted to ask you some more about the race and your impressions when you found Ms. Parker in Ms. Worthington's room."

"Pepper's last name is Worthington?"

"Stella Worthington. She's the daughter of Collins Worthington the Third."

"Collins Worthington as in Worthington Aeronautics?"

"One and the same. So tell me about the race."

"Have you confirmed that the person who died in the crash is Pepper—or Stella I should say, I guess?" I asked, totally ignoring Salinger's question.

"The body was burned beyond recognition, but it appears to be the woman who went by the name of Pepper. We know that the person who died in the crash was female, approximately the same age and height as Ms. Worthington. We found a necklace around the victim's neck that one of the other drivers told one of the deputies Pandora had given to Pepper for her birthday. So back to my question: tell me everything," he emphasized, "about the race."

I settled in for a long visit. "Yesterday, Pandora and Boomer and I met for lunch to discuss the derby. Boomer and Pandora had very different ideas about how the competition should be handled in terms of merging or segregating the men and the women. They came up with the idea for the road race. The winner was to decide the outcome of the debate."

Salinger narrowed his eyes and glared at me. "Road racing is illegal," he pointed out.

"I know. I tried to talk them out of it, but they were determined to follow through with the idea."

"You realize I can have you arrested for participating?"

There was the grumpy old sheriff I knew and loved.

"Really?" I asked. "I'm willingly sitting here missing lunch with Levi and Pandora to answer your questions and you're seriously going to threaten me with some bogus arrest?"

"No." Salinger sighed. "I apologize. I guess old habits are hard to break. Continue with your story."

It's odd; not too long ago I had been feeling responsible for what had happened, and now I was just feeling defensive. I guess blaming yourself for an unfortunate incident is different from having someone else blame you.

"Anyway," I continued, "they wanted me to show up to act as judge. I arrived at 5:20, as instructed. Everyone who was expected to be there was except for Pandora. I figured she just wanted to make a grand entrance, so I wasn't concerned until it was just a few minutes before the start time and she still hadn't arrived. I was about to declare a forfeit when she rolled up in her pink car. At least, I thought it was her."

"And you couldn't tell that the driver wasn't Ms. Parker?"

"No. Pandora is petite, as is Pepper. The driver wore a full racing suit, as well as a full helmet that covered her head and face. I had no reason to believe it wasn't Pandora in the car, so to be honest, I didn't look that hard."

"And then what happened?"

"Levi started the race and in a few seconds it was over. Pandora won by a bumper and all the women began to cheer, but instead of stopping, the car continued on toward the cliff, disappeared around the corner, and then plunged over the side. I called 911 and you showed up."

Salinger handed me a pen and paper. "I want you to list everyone who was there, as well as any general impressions you can remember about each spectator."

"Impressions?"

"Were they angry, happy, drunk? Were they part of a crowd or did they stand off to the side? Who was at the finish line and who remained at the start? Who talked or argued with whom? That sort of thing."

"That will take a while," I pointed out.

"I have time."

Terrific.

"I think you should consider the fact that Pandora was intentionally drugged so that she'd miss the race," I said as I began to write.

"I'd thought of that," Salinger informed me. "We drew some blood while she was here. I put a rush on it, so we should have preliminary findings back soon, although a full panel will take longer. I suspect, based on her description of what happened, that she was slipped some sort of tranquilizer with the intention of knocking her out."

"So one of the guys most likely wanted her to miss the race," I concluded.

"Perhaps. Have you noticed any specific tension between Ms. Parker and any of the other contestants?"

"Boomer and Pandora fight a lot, but I don't think Boomer would drug her. There are a few new men participating this year. I don't really know any of them well, but it did occur to me that if someone drugged Pandora to stop the race and they had reason to believe they were successful, they might not have bothered to get up early to attend the race. I made a list of the contestants that weren't there."

"Please leave those names as well. Anything else about the race that stands out?" Salinger asked.

"No, not that I can think of at the moment."

"Okay, so on to the discovery that Ms. Parker wasn't dead. What led you to look for her in Ms. Worthington's room?"

"Actually, I was looking for Pepper. She hadn't been at the race and no one had been able to find her since. Willa was interviewing the contestants to find out who was still in for tomorrow's competition and who was out. She hadn't been able to locate Pepper or Dezee. It's my job to rework the groups with the remaining contestants, so I was motivated to track Pepper down. I went to her room and knocked, but there was no answer. The door was open, so I went inside and found Pandora in the bed."

"That must have been a shock."

"A bit," I admitted. I left out the part about screaming like a girl.

"And what happened after you realized Ms. Parker was alive?"

I filled Salinger in on the conversation I'd had with Pandora, as well as my general impression that she had no idea what had happened and really didn't seem to remember much since the previous evening.

"Sheriff Salinger . . ." The voice of the receptionist, who must have finally reappeared, came over the intercom, interrupting me just as I got to the part where I convinced Pandora to talk to him.

"Yes?"

"Impound yard on line one. They say it's important."

"Please excuse me." Salinger picked up the line, barked out his name, and listened. His frown deepened the longer he was on the line. I assumed the news wasn't to his liking. He put down the phone and looked at me.

"It looks as though our accident wasn't an accident after all."

Chapter 7

"What do you mean, it wasn't an accident?" I asked.

"The car had been tampered with. Even if Ms. Parker had been driving, the outcome would have been the same. It seems that someone wanted to do more than just stop the race. Someone went to a lot of trouble to make sure that the car ended up at the bottom of the cliff."

"So who was the intended victim?" I had to wonder. "Pandora or Pepper?"

Salinger frowned. I could tell he hadn't considered the fact that Pepper might have been the one someone wanted to kill.

"I don't suppose that whoever tampered with the vehicle had any way of knowing that Ms. Worthington would be driving the car, so the intended victim must have been Ms. Parker," Salinger said.

"Unless whoever tampered with the car is also the one who drugged Pandora, thereby ensuring that she wouldn't be driving the vehicle at the time of the race."

"Yes, but how would the killer have known that Ms. Worthington would take it upon herself to take Ms. Parker's place?" Salinger asked.

"True."

It did seem odd that Pepper hadn't approached one of the other women more experienced with road racing to take Pandora's place once she realized that Pandora was never going to make it in time.

"It looks like this case has just gotten a whole lot more complicated, and Ms. Worthington's parents are on their way back from overseas. I'd like to have some answers for them when they arrive in," Salinger looked at his watch, "twelve hours."

"I'll snoop around and see what I can find out from the other contestants while you find out what happened to the car and how exactly Pandora was drugged."

"You do realize that this is a police matter?" Salinger pointed out. "I should be the one making plans."

"Do you want my help or not?"

Salinger hesitated. I knew he hated the fact that he really did need my help. "If you hear anything, let me know," he answered without committing to the help thing one way or the other.

I called Levi, who was still at Ellie's with Pandora. I told him that I had news and they should wait there for me to arrive. After a bit of discussion, it was decided that it might be better to talk in a less public place, so we arranged to meet at the boathouse as soon as they finished their meal. I called Zak to fill him in. I didn't want to interfere with his time at the beach, but I also didn't want him to think I was leaving him out of what had just turned into another Zoe Donovan murder investigation.

I also checked in with Jeremy, who said he was fine and didn't need me to come in.

I started reworking the derby schedule while I waited for Levi and Pandora. It occurred to me that

Boomer most likely still didn't know that Pandora was alive. I realized that his reaction to the news could be pretty telling, so I called Levi again and told him I might be a few minutes late, and then headed to the park downtown where the cars were displayed for viewers as well as potential buyers.

I suspected Boomer would be at the car show with the other members of his team, but when I stopped by, I was informed by Masher that Boomer had pulled out of the entire event and planned to leave the area as soon as he was packed. I changed direction and headed over to the Ashton Falls Motor Inn. I knocked on the door of his room and was invited to come on inside.

"Hey, Zoe." Boomer sounded defeated. "Guess you heard I was leaving."

"I did, although I'm surprised, given the circumstances."

"Circumstances?"

I watched his face as I continued to speak. "I figured that once you found out that Pandora didn't die in the crash this morning, you'd stay around to help her deal with things."

Boomer's jaw dropped. "What do you mean, she didn't die? Of course she died. There's no way anyone could have survived that crash."

"True, but Pandora wasn't driving the car. I thought you knew that."

Boomer grabbed my arm. Hard. "Are you messing with me?"

"Of course not. Now let me go, you oaf."

I pulled my arm away and began rubbing it. I was pretty sure I was going to have a bruise.

"Pandora wasn't driving?"

I could see that he wanted to believe me but couldn't quite bring himself to do so.

"She wasn't," I insisted. "I've talked to her myself. She was passed out in bed when I found her. Guess she had too much to drink last night."

Boomer smiled as he let my news sink in. "Then who?" He left the sentence unfinished, but I knew what he was asking.

"Pepper."

Boomer's smile turned back into a frown. "Pepper? Why Pepper?"

"I guess she decided to fill in for Pandora so the race wouldn't be forfeited."

Boomer sat down on his bed and put his head in his hands. I decided to give him a minute to process things. He seemed genuinely surprised that Pandora was alive and Pepper was dead. It didn't clear him from tampering with the car or drugging Pandora, but I got the feeling he was almost as torn up about Pepper as he had been about Pandora. If I had to guess, Boomer was innocent of both acts.

"God, poor Pepper," Boomer groaned. "The whole thing makes no sense. I was with Pandora last night. She had two drinks, maybe three. Definitely not enough to get drunk."

"Did you notice her acting oddly?"

Boomer lifted his head, ran his hand through his thick dark hair, and looked at the ceiling. "This whole thing is my fault," he moaned.

"Your fault?"

"I did notice Pandora was acting strange, but I figured she was just tired. I'd had a few drinks before she arrived and was feeling the effect of the alcohol. I remember telling her to go back to her room and sleep it off. I should have known something was off."

"Did Pandora leave with Pepper?" I asked.

"No, Pepper had already gone. Pandora left with Dezee. He said he'd walk her back to her room since he was going out for a smoke. These are all nonsmoking rooms."

"Have you seen Dezee today?"

I knew he hadn't been at the race, and Willa hadn't tracked him down as of this morning's emergency events committee meeting.

"No, I haven't," Boomer answered. "He must be at the show with the guys."

"He's not. I was just there, looking for you."

Boomer frowned.

"Do you have any idea where he might be?" I asked.

"No idea at all. Dezee has been saving up for a new muscle car. He has enough if he can get a good-enough price at the auction for his old Nova. I know he was looking forward to showing her off during the weekend events. Are you sure he wasn't in town?"

I hadn't noticed him, but I really hadn't looked around all that much, so I couldn't be sure he wasn't there.

"How about we go and take a look? I need to confirm with everyone who is in and who is out for tomorrow's derby anyway. After that, you can come with me to meet Pandora and Levi, if you'd like."

Dezee wasn't at the park, and no one had seen him since the previous evening. Everyone decided to participate in the derby as planned, although Boomer wanted to talk to Pandora before committing. By the time we got to the boathouse, Levi and Pandora were waiting on the back deck.

"You live here?" Boomer asked as we pulled up.

"I do."

"Wow, it's great. I bet you have a fantastic view."

I nodded. "Let's grab a couple of beers and join the others."

The reunion between Boomer and Pandora was sweet. I'm pretty sure they both had tears running down their faces as they hugged and once and for all put to bed any doubt I might have had that they were more than rivals.

"I'm sorry about Pepper," Boomer said to Pandora. "I know she was like a sister to you. I can't imagine what might have possessed her to take your car and fill in for you. She's an okay derby driver, but she wasn't a drag racer."

"She must have realized I wasn't going to make it and wanted to fill in," Pandora said sadly.

"Yeah, but why didn't she ask Jugs or Zelda to take over?" Boomer said, stating the same thought I'd had earlier. "They have experience with road racing, and we both know Pepper only joined your team to be close to you. She just pulled right up to the starting line. Why wouldn't she enlist the help of the others? The whole thing makes no sense."

Pandora frowned. "Boomer is right. Pepper would have brought the car to the starting point if she realized I wasn't going to make it, but she wouldn't have raced herself." Pandora looked at me. "You said that Jugs and Zelda were both at the race?"

"Yes, they were both there," I confirmed. "To be honest, I had a similar thought when I learned that the victim was Pepper."

"There has to be more to this," Pandora insisted.

"There are a couple of pieces to the story that may or may not be related," I pointed out. "First of all, it appears that you were drugged last night, Pandora. We won't have confirmation until Salinger gets the blood test back, but based on what everyone has said, a couple of drinks wouldn't render you unconscious.

"Additionally," I added, "we know that the car was tampered with, ensuring a fiery conclusion to the race. The person who tampered with the car may or may not have been involved in the drugging incident.

"And finally, we know that Pepper, for whatever reason, decided to participate in the race personally rather than asking for help from more qualified team members. Perhaps she wanted to protect your reputation with the others." I looked at Pandora.

"Maybe, but I still think she would have filled in Jugs at the very least. Jugs has been part of the team for a long time. Pepper would know that she wouldn't think less of me, even if I had been dumb enough to get wasted the night before a race."

"Seems like we have a lot of questions," Levi added. "Was Pandora drugged? If so, by whom and why? Who tampered with the car and why? Why did Pepper decide to race rather than enlisting the help of the more-qualified Jugs? If a fiery crash was the intention of whoever tampered with the car, who was the intended victim?"

"Yeah, and where is Dezee?" Boomer added. "I know that participating in the show in town was really important to him. It makes no sense that he'd miss it."

"Unless he's our guilty party," I speculated.

"Dezee?" Boomer appeared shocked by my suggestion.

"Dezee would never do anything to hurt anyone," Pandora agreed. "He's good friends with Pepper, so I've gotten to know him well over the past six months. He's a good guy. Sweet and gentle."

"Okay, so if you had to guess, who do you think *would* have wanted to drug Pandora and/or cause the crash?" I asked.

Boomer and Pandora both seemed to be pondering my question. Chances were that the guilty party or parties were involved in the classic car show in some capacity. Some random person not connected to the show was a possibility, but it seemed like a long shot at best.

My phone rang as Levi and I waited for Boomer and Pandora to offer some suggestion as to where we might begin our investigation.

It was Salinger.

"The prelims for the blood test are back. It confirmed that Pandora was given a tranquilizer. It appears she was slipped a drug called Rohypnol, a sedative more commonly known as a roofie. The drug was most likely added to her drink. I'm going to need the names of everyone she was partying with last night."

"I'll get it and call you back," I assured him.

"Get what?" Pandora asked.

I explained about the drug. Both Pandora and Boomer hit the ceiling when they realized that someone they were close to had drugged the derby diva and most likely was at least partially responsible for Pepper's death. I got them calmed down and managed to get the list Salinger was looking for.

Chapter 8

"So after Boomer and Pandora compared notes, they came up with a list of eight names, including their own," I informed Zak later that evening as I recounted the events of the day. Scooter was inside playing video games, while Zak and I shared a bottle of wine on his lakeside deck. Charlie was sleeping at my feet and Bella slept at Zak's side. I was happy to see that the dog had settled right in.

"Boomer, Pandora, Pepper, Dezee, Jugs, Masher, Rizo, and Big Boy Branson were all at the impromptu party," I continued. "We know it wasn't Boomer or Pandora and are fairly certain it wasn't Pepper, which leaves Dezee, Jugs, Masher, Rizo, and Big Boy Branson."

"Who seems most likely?" Zak asked as he tossed another log on the fire he'd built in the outdoor pit.

"Dezee has been missing since last night, so he seems the strongest suspect to me, but Boomer and Pandora both insist he wouldn't have done it. Jugs has been touring with Pandora for a long time and next to Pepper is probably her best friend, so it seems unlikely she'd drug her. Masher is Boomer's number two and wouldn't have acted without Boomer's consent, so the pair agreed we could eliminate him as well. That leaves Rizo and Big Boy. Rizo is a quintessential dumb blonde. I doubt she'd be one to come up with some sort of master plan, so my money at this point is on Big Boy Branson."

"Do all the car people have strange nicknames?" Zak wondered.

"No, not really. The derby drivers tend to either choose nicknames or they're given to them by their competitors. Those who don't race but merely display their cars and participate in the parade and auction don't always have nicknames. The Pencil Triplets are only referred to as such because no one can tell them apart."

"Okay, back to Big Boy Branson. Have you managed to come up with a motive for him to drug Pandora?"

"No," I admitted. "Boomer and Pandora are going to talk to him. We decided that they would conduct an investigation of sorts from the inside, while I snooped around on the outside. Levi is going to help me since you're tied up with Scooter and Ellie is totally booked between work and dating."

"I see she didn't drag you into tonight's event."

"No, thank God. I told her I was out of the dating game for good and she could find another wingman."

"For good?" Zak smiled.

"Yeah. I guess we should talk about that."

"Later. After I get Scooter off to bed."

I found that I was both excited about and terrified of the pending conversation.

"So what about the others?" Zak asked.

"Others?"

"If whoever drugged Pandora was working with someone else as part of a bigger plan, then whoever tampered with the car might have done so while everyone else was partying."

"Good point." I thought about who hadn't been there and started another list. "Assuming we limit the suspect pool to those involved in the derby, there are eight other contestants. If the list I got from Boomer and Pandora is accurate, the only two females not present at the party were Jaqui and Zelda. Jaqui isn't much of a joiner, so I don't find it odd that she wasn't there. She's very driven and, as far as I can tell, very capable of tampering with the car. If it turned out to be her, I guess I wouldn't be completely surprised, but I don't see her working as part of a team. She's a very hard woman who isn't easy to get to know. I'm pretty sure she grew up in some sort of gang."

"Why do you say that?" Zak asked.

"She has this very tough way about her and seems to be distrustful of pretty much everyone. She walks around with a knife strapped to her leg, and although I've never seen her use it, she has a presence that lets you know she *has* used it in the past and isn't afraid to use it again."

"And what about Zelda?"

"Zelda is big and strong and knows a lot about cars. This is her first year as a contender in the derby, but I met her last year, when she participated in the car show. I don't know that she *would* tamper with the car, but I'm fairly certain she'd be capable of rigging one to crash at an opportune moment if she were so inclined."

"Did you ever find out exactly what happened?" Zak asked. "Did the brakes fail? The steering?"

"They're still looking into it, but it appears that the brake line was slit, causing brake fluid to leak out slowly, which is why Pepper could have driven the car from town to the race with no problem. Unfortunately, the leak created a total failure of the brakes at the worst time."

"Sounds like sophisticated tampering," Zak observed.

"Yeah, these car people know their stuff."

"What about the guys who weren't at the party?"

"Of the men, Crusher, the Pencil Triplets, Bruiser, and Crank weren't present. The Pencil Triplets tend to keep to themselves, so it isn't surprising that they weren't partying with the others. Bruiser and Crank are new this year, so they probably don't know the others. Crusher has been hanging with Boomer for quite some time, so it's a little odd that he wasn't partying with the others. I asked Boomer about it, and he said it was his impression that Crusher might have been busy hooking up with a woman, possibly Zelda, since she was missing as well."

"This reminds me of the mystery we were faced with at Charles Tisdale's farm last Thanksgiving. Limited suspects, but each seems to have his or her own story."

"We figured that one out and we'll figure this one out too," I said with more confidence than I felt. "So exactly what time does Scooter go to bed?"

"Strike two," Ellie complained in my ear as I listened to her tell me about her date while I waited for Zak to come back outside after putting Scooter to bed.

"I told you this wasn't going to be easy," I reminded her.

"I know, but these guys all seem so great when we're chatting online, and then I meet them in person and it all falls apart."

"So what went wrong?" I asked. I was pretty sure I already knew but felt it was polite to ask anyway.

"It started off okay. He took me to a nice restaurant and we chatted over a bottle of wine and an appetizer while we waited for our table to be ready. He told me about his job and his hobbies and I told him about mine. I thought everything was going really well until he faked a phone call and promptly informed me that he had an emergency and had to leave before we were even seated for our meal."

"Did the subject of children come up?" I cringed as I waited for her reply.

"I guess, in a roundabout sort of way," Ellie admitted.

"How roundabout are we talking?"

"He was telling me about his plans to travel to Europe next winter and asked if I was interested in traveling. I mentioned that I hoped to be pregnant by next winter, so I wasn't making any plans that far in advance, but that, in theory, I loved the idea of traveling."

Ouch.

"Sweetie, you know I love you and I want you to be happy, but you're never going to have a second date with *anyone* if you keep bringing up pregnancy and kids."

"I just don't want to waste any time on some guy who doesn't want kids."

I took a deep breath and said a quick prayer that I could come up with something helpful to say that wouldn't make Ellie mad.

"I know that having a baby is the most important thing to you. And I understand that dating a man for even a few weeks who isn't interested in having children seems like a waste of time. But even men who want children generally don't want to discuss the possibility on a first date. I think that in general, most people—men and women—want to know you're interested in *them*, not just in their baby-making abilities."

Ellie sighed. "I see your point."

"I'm sorry this guy didn't work out. Maybe the next one will."

"I do have a message in my in-box. I guess I can see who it's from. I was just so sure that this guy would be the one."

"I know. I'm sorry this is so hard for you. I wish I was as skilled at finding perfect matches between men and women as I am between animals and humans."

Ellie gasped. "Of course! I should have you pick my next date. You really are a genius at matching people and animals, so why not humans?"

"That's not what I was implying," I backpedaled.

"Please," Ellie said persuasively. "Just give it a try."

"I wouldn't know where to start."

"Let's meet for lunch tomorrow and we can discuss it. I'll bring my laptop and we can look at the guys on the dating site."

I wanted to help Ellie, but I didn't want to get in the middle of her dating frenzy.

"Tomorrow is the first round of the derby. I'm going to be pretty busy."

"You're the one who wanted me to date rather than pursuing a sperm donor," Ellie reminded me.

"I never said you should engage in marathon dating," I pointed out. "I just wanted you to wait before making such a huge decision."

Ellie sighed again, and I felt like a total heel. She had been there so many times for me. Even when she was busy, she always made time to help me through the endless personal crises I'd seemed to attract pre-Zak.

"Okay," I agreed. "The derby is in the afternoon, so how about an early lunch? I can't promise anything, but I'll do my best to pick out a good one."

"Thank you. I love you. I'll see you tomorrow."

"Pick out a good what?" Zak asked as he rejoined me.

"Man."

"Come again?"

I laughed. "For Ellie, not me. It seems I'm going into the matchmaking business."

"Do you think that's a good idea?"

"Not in the least. In fact, I think it's a terrible idea that I will live to regret."

Zak frowned at me. "So why do it?"

I shrugged. "You know me. I'm a glutton for punishment."

Zak kissed my neck. "Scooter is asleep and if you want to be punished . . ."

I kissed him back as his hands wandered up my back. I had a feeling our very important talk was going to have to wait for another day.

Chapter 9

Friday, July 11

As promised, everyone on the events committee met at 7 a.m., which came *very* early after the late night Zak and I had shared. We never had gotten around to talking, but after the intimacy of the evening, I was finally convinced that things really were going to be okay. I realized somewhere around two a.m. that I needed to sit down alone to figure out exactly why I was hesitating to make Zak a permanent part of my life. I knew that emotionally he'd been just that for quite some time, yet I was hesitant to commit to a formal arrangement. Maybe I was more like my mother than I cared to admit. I'd been raised by my dad, so you wouldn't think that her flighty nature would have rubbed off on me, but here I was, repeating the mistakes of the woman who bore me.

"Why so serious?" Ellie asked as she sat down next to me with her own Styrofoam cup of coffee. Ellie looked as tired and distracted as I did, and I imagined that she most likely had suffered through her own long night of self-evaluation and introspection.

"I was just wondering if I'm destined to repeat the mistakes of my mother."

"Why would you think that? You're nothing like your mother."

I looked at Ellie.

"Okay, you *are* a little like your mother, but I don't see you taking off when things get intense."

"Maybe not physically but emotionally . . ."

Ellie paused to take a bite of her doughnut. She chewed slowly and swallowed before answering. I hadn't planned to eat any of the sugary treats laid out for us, but Ellie's chocolate bar with cream filling looked delicious.

"I guess you've inherited some of your mother's issues with commitment, but in the end you always face your fears and stay," Ellie insisted. "I don't know why it's so hard for you to accept the commitment Zak wants to make with you, but I can't imagine you packing up and leaving either."

"Yeah." I smiled. "I guess you're right. I really should just accept Zak's proposal and quit stressing over something I don't even understand."

"Really?"

"Sure," I decided. "But I should probably tell Zak yes before I tell you yes, so how about we keep this to ourselves for now?"

Ellie hugged me. "I'm so happy for you."

I hugged her back. "I'm happy for me too."

"So about finding me a guy . . ." Ellie brought the conversation back around to my promise of the previous evening.

I'd hoped Ellie had reconsidered her request. What did I know about picking out a man for a woman with a ticking biological clock? My own biological clock was moving at a glacial speed, which was just fine with me. I had to wonder about Zak's biological clock, however. If men even had biological clocks. He sure did seem to be having fun with Scooter, and I couldn't help but wonder if that wasn't going to bring to the forefront thoughts of having his own child. Our child.

Yikes.

Here I was, freaking myself out again. *Breathe, Zoe. Just breathe.*

"I'm sure Willa has chores for us this morning, and I should check in with Jeremy." I decided to focus on Ellie's dilemma in order to get my mind off my own crazy thoughts. "I never did go by the Zoo yesterday. I know you're supposed to help Tawny with the food, so let's get together before the main lunch crowd arrives. Maybe eleven?"

"Eleven sounds perfect. I'll bring my laptop. I spent some time last night selecting men who live within a sixty-mile radius and I happen to find attractive. I've narrowed it down to five men, so all you have to do is look at the five and figure out which one will work best as my prince charming."

"And if none of them really fits the bill?"

Ellie frowned. "Is it supposed to be this hard?"

"No, it's supposed to be easy, but if you want my honest opinion, I think you're making it hard. Zak and I should never have found each other. I didn't even like him, and I certainly wasn't trying to make things happen with him. They just did. I promised to help you and I will if you want me to, but I really think you should just let nature take its course."

Ellie took a sip of her what by this point must be tepid coffee as she appeared to be considering my suggestion. I watched as a myriad of emotions crossed her face. I knew she was struggling with this whole thing, and while I wanted to understand, I was having a hard time getting to a point where I could empathize with her urgency.

"Nature is slow," Ellie decided. "I want a baby now."

"See, that's exactly what I'm afraid of. You aren't looking for a life partner but a man to have children with. I honestly feel like you're setting yourself up for heartache."

I was sure Ellie knew I was right about this, but I didn't think she wanted to acknowledge the fact that sometimes important things operated on their own timetables.

"So maybe I should just skip the man and get right to the baby, like I was going to do before you talked me into trying to find a man to have a baby with."

"No." I sighed. "That is not what I'm saying at all. Have you considered a puppy?"

"A puppy?"

"Yeah. Having a puppy to practice being a mother with is actually a good idea. You miss spending time with Hannah and you're trying to replace what you had with her, but having a baby will be hard. You won't be able to come and go like you do now, and you certainly won't be able to work the long hours that are required to get a new business off the ground. Please think about what I'm saying."

"I don't mind hard, and a puppy is not a baby," Ellie insisted. "By the way, where is your puppy?"

"Charlie is with Zak and Scooter. What I meant was that a puppy would be easier than a baby, yet it would still provide companionship. Having a baby on your own isn't going to be as easy as you think."

"Other people do it," Ellie said.

"Sure, but most single parents really struggle."

I could see that try as I might, I wasn't getting through to a woman who had already made up her mind.

"What about Jeremy? He's raising Morgan on his own and he seems to be doing fine."

Ellie had a point. Jeremy did seem to be doing fine, but he had a lot of help from friends and neighbors.

"Do me a favor and talk to Jeremy about it. *Really* talk to him, and get him to tell you the good and the bad. If you still want to have a baby on your own after talking to him, I'll help you."

"Oh, all right," Ellie reluctantly agreed. "I don't think he can say anything to change my mind, but if my talking to him will make you happy, I'll do it."

"Thank you. I appreciate that. Now about that puppy . . ."

Ellie laughed. "Let me guess: you have some little darling who needs a home and you're trying to work your mojo on me so I'll adopt him or her?"

"No, I don't currently have a puppy I'm trying to place, but a puppy would provide you with a friend to come home to."

"I thought I was going to be coming home to you and Charlie. Did you forget that I'm moving in with you until I find a place?"

Actually, with everything that had been going on, I *had* temporarily forgotten.

"Of course I haven't forgotten," I assured her. "I'm very excited that you're going to be staying with us. I just meant that you might want to adopt a puppy after you find a place."

Ellie looked at me skeptically. We'd been friends too long for me to try to pull something over on her and we both knew it.

By the time I got to the Zoo, it was after nine, and I had to leave by 10:45 to meet Ellie, so I needed to get focused if I was going to get anything done at all. The first round of the derby was that afternoon, so I doubted I'd be back once I left. As I pulled up to the log building that was designed to house both wild and domestic animals, I smiled. I smile every time I pull up to the large building that I love. There had been a few people in my life who hadn't understood my total commitment to the animals with which we share the earth. I'm not sure why I decided to commit my life to rescuing and rehabilitating these wonderful creatures, but doing it gave me a feeling of contentment that I was certain nothing else could replace.

"Okay, fill me in," I instructed Jeremy the moment I walked in the door. He was feeding the baby raccoons that had been dropped off the previous weekend. "I'm afraid I don't have a lot of time this morning."

"How about you fill me in first?" he suggested as he used an eyedropper to complete his task. "I heard Pandora Parker isn't dead after all."

I quickly explained what I knew to Jeremy, which wasn't a lot at that point. "Hopefully, something will happened today to give us a little focus. Right now, there are just too many possibilities to make sense of the whole thing."

"Like what?" Jeremy wondered as he returned the baby raccoons to the cage closest to the office, which was where we'd decided to keep them. They really were cute little things, although I wondered what had become of their mother.

"Like whether the fact that Pandora was drugged and the fact that her car was tampered with are related." I began sorting the mail on my desk as we talked.

"Aren't they?" Jeremy asked as he returned to my office.

"Not necessarily." I tossed a flyer for commercial dog food into the trash. "I know it seems like they must be, but the more I think about it, the less certain I am that the two things are connected at all."

"If they aren't, you have two bad guys," Jeremy said. "Seems unlikely."

"Maybe, but the drugging and the car tampering aren't the only strange things that had to occur for everything to play out the way it did."

"What do you mean?"

I sat down in my desk chair and faced Jeremy, who had taken a seat in one of the folding chairs I'd placed along one wall for prospective animal parents to use while they filled out the paperwork I required.

"Someone drugged Pandora *and* someone tampered with her car. If Pandora was the target of the tampering, why drug her, thereby ensuring that she'd be too messed up to drive? If the intended victim of the tampering was Pepper, whoever did the tampering would have had to have had reason to believe she would take Pandora's place in the race, but both Pandora and Boomer felt that her doing so was very out of character."

Jeremy frowned as he appeared to consider the situation.

"Okay, I can see how things aren't really lining up," Jeremy decided. "Any suspects?"

"Dezee's actions seem suspicious in nature, although as of the last time I spoke to Boomer and Pandora, he's still missing. No one can imagine where he got off to. He didn't take his car or his things from his room, so they're operating on the assumption that he didn't just leave."

"It does seem like if he was guilty and wanted to get gone, he'd take his stuff with him," Jeremy agreed. "I guess the whole thing *is* pretty murky."

"It really is. So back to my question: what has been going on around here?"

"Winnie called," Jeremy began. "She's all settled into her new place but wanted to check on Bella. I told her she was very happy in her new home, but I think she wants you to call her."

"I will and she is. Happy in her new home," I clarified. "What else?"

"One of the bears we released last fall was found digging through one of the Dumpsters in town. Fish and Game want to relocate her to another area, since she's returned to the scene of the crime more than once, and they wanted to know if we could keep her until they can arrange a relocation. I told them yes, and she's currently napping in the big-cat cage because we still have the Anderson fire cubs in the cub cage."

"Sounds like you did exactly what I would have. Go on."

"Tiffany and I have been stopping by the campground where they're doing the cleanup of the contaminated groundwater. During our conversations with the crew working on the project, we've learned that they suspect the contamination came from a broken sewer line rather than deliberate dumping, as we originally suspected. The thing is, just cleaning up the water in the campground isn't going to do any good in the long run unless they can find the leak, so we could be looking at a lengthy process. Salinger closed the campground, which caused quite a stir with the owner and the campers, but to be honest, the area is beginning to take on an unpleasant stench, so I'm betting the campers would have been making other arrangements anyway."

"I'll bet. It really is too bad the whole thing had to happen during the summer. It'll be hard for the campground owner to make up his losses if he doesn't have the right insurance. I guess we should be looking for other sick animals. If the water is coming from the sewer and there's a leak, we might find other locations where the sewer water and groundwater have mixed and risen to the surface."

I hated to think about the wide-range damage such a scenario could cause. The dead squirrels in the campground had been discovered quickly because the deaths had occurred in a highly populated area, but if there was contamination in a less-populated location, there could be a lot of victims before the problem was discovered.

"The guys from the public utility district are going to work on tracking down the leak, but it would be best if we could find the source of the toxic chemicals."

"The meth lab," I concluded.

"Exactly. Salinger is pretty occupied with this murder case, so I'm thinking the meth lab is going to take a backseat."

Jeremy wasn't wrong.

"You remember my friend Spike?"

"Yeah." I nodded. Spike was a member of the metal band Jeremy had belonged to before his daughter was born.

"Well, he used to dabble in certain forms of illegal stimulants."

Knowing what I knew about Spike, I wasn't surprised.

"He told me that there's a guy in the area who's known for producing a significant quantity of the stuff. He has some kind of degree in chemistry and when he couldn't find a decent job, he decided to become an entrepreneur."

"Entrepreneur?"

"The term fits," Jeremy insisted.

"Yeah, I guess it does. Go on. I'm assuming you're pulling up to a point?"

"No one knows where this guy gets his product, but Spike thinks he has a lab in one of the wilderness cabins near Grainger's Peak."

"The wilderness cabins aren't hooked up to the sewer system, so a lab in one of the cabins wouldn't be causing the problem we're having."

"True," Jeremy said, "but Spike says the guy is a real environmentalist."

I frowned. A drug dealer with an environmental conscious?

"Anyway, Spike's theory is that he's producing the stuff in one of the cabins and then disposing of the waste in the sewer."

"Have you told Salinger?"

"Not yet. Spike didn't want me to reveal how he knows about this particular lab. I was thinking I might take a hike out there to see what I can see. If I find a cabin that I suspect may contain the lab, I'll let Salinger know."

"No way," I insisted. "Snooping around looking for a meth lab is dangerous. I'm going to tell Salinger about the cabin theory and let him look into it. I won't mention either you or Spike."

"Okay," Jeremy agreed somewhat reluctantly.

"You have Morgan to think about. She needs you, so don't be a hero."

"I said I'd let you handle it."

"Good. Hopefully, Salinger will look into it right away. In the meantime, if other animals start turning up dead, let me know."

"I will."

"And if Spike is involved with this chemist in any way, you might tell him to keep a low profile."

"Spike is clean now, but I'll give him a heads-up. By the way, I heard your mom and dad are getting married."

"They are, but how did you know?"

"Your dad called me. He said you suggested I provide the music, and he wanted to be sure I could play something other than metal."

"I'm sorry. I was supposed to talk to you about it, but with everything that's happened . . ."

"Don't worry about it. Morgan and I are going over to your parents' for dinner. I'm going to bring my guitar so we can preview songs."

"Harper and Morgan are having a playdate and I'm going to miss it?"

"Zoe, they're three months old. I doubt they'll be doing much playing."

"Yeah, but I bet they'll be so cute together. I'm going to the parade and chili cook-off with Zak and Scooter, but I'll try to stop by for a minute. What time are you going over?"

"Six."

I didn't think my biological clock was ticking, but just thinking about Harper and Morgan lying next to each other on a blanket made me all gooey inside. Maybe Ellie wasn't as crazy as I thought.

Then I remembered the disastrous double date.

Or maybe she was.

"Listen, Jeremy, I wanted to talk to you about Ellie."

"What's up with her?"

I explained about her almost manic drive to have a baby no matter what the circumstances. I was really worried about her and hoped Jeremy could shed some light on the hardships that came with bringing another person into the world and trying to raise them on your own.

"When I found out Gina was pregnant with Morgan, I was scared," Jeremy said. "I was just a kid. What did I know about raising a baby? I talked myself into believing it would be easy, but you're correct in the fact that it's hard. Very hard at times. But to be honest, having Morgan in my life is the best thing that ever could have happened to me. If I had it to do over again, I would. She has given meaning and texture to my life that I didn't even know I was missing. I know you're worried about Ellie going it alone, but if there was ever anyone cut out to be a mother, it's her."

I frowned. I'd sort of hoped he'd tell me how hard it was to deal with midnight feedings, colic, messy diapers, and a total loss of freedom. Jeremy was only twenty-one, yet he seemed really happy and honestly content.

"I'll talk to Ellie," Jeremy offered. "I do agree that hooking up with some random guy just to have a baby isn't the way to go."

"Thanks, Jeremy. I'm supposed to meet her for lunch, but if you want to go in my stead, I'll keep an eye on things here."

"I'd be happy to, as long as you call her and tell her about the switch."

"Done."

Chapter 10

We ended up with fourteen entries for the preliminary round, five women and nine men. I decided to simply create two groups of seven, with the final three from each group going on to the finals the following day. The trick was going to not only be one of the last three cars running but to be in good enough shape to compete in the finals. Since Pepper had technically won the race, it was decided that the groups would be coed, as originally voted on by the committee.

I made certain that Boomer and Pandora were put into different groups. Other than that, I randomly picked two women and four men for each of the two groups. Up first was the group that consisted of Pandora, Jaqui, Rizo, Masher, two of the Pencil Triplets, and Bruiser. The second group would be Boomer, Jugs, Zelda, Crusher, the third Pencil Triplet, Crank, and Big Boy Branson.

"I thought the mood would be somber after what happened to Pepper," Levi commented, "but there's an explosive energy like always."

"Most of the people in the crowd didn't even know Pepper. I think the crash has actually made the whole weekend somehow more exciting for the average derby spectator. And those drivers who were close to Pepper are looking at the derby as a sort of stress relief. I'm predicting that the crashes will be more explosive than normal. I just hope we have three cars from each group left in good enough condition to compete tomorrow."

"And if we don't?"

I shrugged. "We'll compete with what we have."

Unlike the cars that had been on display in town and had participated in the classic car parade, the derby cars were old and heavy, with all the glass removed and roll-over bars installed. Although powerful vehicles, the cars were cosmetically challenged. Still, in spite of the dents that had been pounded out more than once, many of the cars, including Pandora's pink Galaxy, had been painted to demonstrate the personality of the driver.

"Did Dezee ever show up?" Levi asked.

"Not so far. It's really strange that he'd just take off unless he was involved in the tampering, but everyone who knows him agrees that he really doesn't seem to be the type to do such a thing."

"Sometimes it's the quiet ones who have something to hide."

"Maybe, but it seems odd that he'd leave everything including his car behind."

"You mentioned that he was close to Pepper. Maybe he knew that Pepper was the one driving Pandora's car and when it crashed he went off to mourn."

"He wasn't at the race."

"That you saw. Can you honestly say that you saw everyone who was there? I know I can't remember every detail of every minute. He might have shown up late."

"Maybe. Here come the drivers."

The cars were already parked at the starting point, within the boundaries of the makeshift derby track we'd set up in one of Old Man Johnson's unused pastures. Traditionally, we'd used the fairgrounds in Bryton Lake, but there had been a scheduling conflict this year that had left the committee scrambling to figure out an alternate venue. When the committee decided to ask Old Man Johnson for permission to use his pasture, I figured there was no way he'd agree, but Hazel, with her diplomatic disposition and a bagful of pastries, had been successful in getting the reclusive man to go along with our plan. If you want my opinion, he'd been regretting that decision ever since.

The drivers, dressed in their colorful racing suits, paraded around the perimeter of the makeshift fence, waving at the crowd before taking their places in their cars in anticipation of the starting gun. Overall, the energy of the crowd was beyond invigorating, although with the addition of the women to the event, there were a lot more catcalls than I'd ever heard at an event like this.

"Is Zak brining Scooter?" Levi asked.

"Yeah." I looked around at the crowd. "He should be here."

I checked my phone. He hadn't texted to say he wasn't going to make it. I knew Zak and Scooter were still working on getting down their timing. Zak had shared the previous evening that if he anticipated that it would take Scooter thirty minutes to accomplish something such as getting ready to go someplace, washing up to eat, or getting ready for bed, you could bet it would actually take twice that long.

"He probably had to park quite a way down the road," Levi said. "I hope he makes it before they begin. These things usually don't take all that long once they get started."

I scanned the crowd again. There were a lot of people crammed into a small area, but Zak was freakishly tall, so I was certain I would be able to pick him out of the crowd.

"I don't seen them," I said as I surveyed the masses. "Oh wait, there they are."

I waved to Zak and Scooter, who were perched on temporary bleachers along the fence line. I would have liked to sit with them, but as a member of the committee, it was my responsibility to sit in the judges' booth and act as an amateur judge while Levi sat next to me to serve as co-judge and announcer. My dad and Paul were busy at the chili cook-off and Ellie and Tawny were in town overseeing the food, and Willa, Hazel, and Gilda had volunteered to be on hand should problems arise.

"You ready?" I asked.

"As I'll ever be."

Levi greeted everyone and then made the announcement for the drivers to start their engines. The crowd roared with enthusiasm, calling out the names of their favorite drivers, as I shot the gun, which was filled with blanks, and the derby got underway.

"Ouch, that must have hurt." Levi grimaced as Pandora rammed into one of the Pencil Triplets, taking him out of the contest within the first minute of the event.

"It looks like Pandora and Jaqui are working as a team, now that Masher took out Rizo," I commented. "It's going to be hard to get to either of them as long as they continue to have each other's back."

"The guys seem to be working alone at this point," Levi said. "Bruiser just took out one of the Triplets and Masher has been ruthless about chasing down Jaqui."

"I suppose we should have made more of an effort to figure out which Triplet is which," I commented. They were driving completely different cars, so it wouldn't have been that hard.

"Yeah. It just seemed easier to refer to them as numbers one, two, and three."

In the end, the final three left standing from group one were Pandora, Jaqui, and Masher. The results really didn't hold any surprises as far as I was concerned. It would be interesting to see who would survive from round two.

"That concludes round one," Levi announced. "We're going to take a break while the damaged cars are removed from the field. The snack bar is open on the far left with cool drinks, hot dogs, and buttery corn on the cob."

"Maybe you should go into showbiz," I teased Levi. "You have a great stage voice."

"Thanks but no thanks. I'm going to get a soda. Want anything?"

"No thanks. I think I'll head over to say hi to Zak and Scooter while we wait to start round two."

I was halfway around the field, walking toward the bleachers where I'd seen Zak and Scooter, when I noticed Salinger heading toward me.

Now what?

"Did you catch the first round of the derby?" I asked politely. After all, I had decided to make an effort to get along with the man, since he seemed to be willing to work with me after all the help I'd provided in the past.

"Sorry I missed it. I called your cell, but when you didn't get back to me, I decided to come out here to find you."

"I'm the official judge, so I turned my phone off. What's up?"

Salinger looked around. There were several hundred people in attendance, although no one seemed to be paying any attention to us.

"Let's go over there in the shade, away from the crowd," he suggested.

I shrugged. Shade sounded good. It was a hot afternoon and the judges' booth had been set up directly under the midday sun. I looked longingly toward the bleachers, where Zak was waiting for me, before following Salinger dutifully across the dusty field that was riddled with gopher holes.

As soon as we arrived at our destination, Salinger began to speak. "It turns out that the body in the morgue isn't Stella Worthington."

"What?" I frowned. "It has to be Pepper. Who else would it be?"

"That's what we're trying to find out. Ms. Worthington's parents arrived from overseas this morning. When we reviewed the coroner's report with them, they pointed out that Pepper had a titanium screw in her shoulder from a dislocation that resulted from a fall from a horse when she was nine. The woman who died in the fire didn't possess such a screw, which would have survived the fire."

I paled. "So if the person who died in the accident wasn't Pepper, who was it?" I realized I was repeating myself, but the news had caught me by surprise. "And if the woman who died wasn't Pepper, where is she?" I added before Salinger could be bothered answering a question he'd already addressed.

"That's what I'm hoping you can help me find out. Ms. Worthington's parents have instructed me not to look for their daughter. They fear she may have been kidnapped and is being held for ransom, though they haven't received any demands so far. They're afraid that if the police become involved, the kidnappers might kill her."

I frowned. "Why do they think that?"

"They're very wealthy people. This is a reality they've had to live with for years. Ms. Worthington chose to go off on her own and join the divas, much to her parents' distress. They provided her with a bodyguard when she lived with them in order to ward off this very situation."

I wiped my forearm across my brow to wipe away the sweat that was beginning to bead. It really was a hot afternoon, and somehow, Salinger's news had made me even more aware of it.

"A bodyguard? Really?" I asked. It seemed sort of extreme.

"I guess the young woman who was hired to protect Ms. Worthington acted as her friend, so as not to make it obvious that she was being protected. According to Mr. Worthington, when Ms. Worthington left home to join the divas, she refused to take her guard with her. Given the fact that she changed her name from Stella Worthington to Pepper, the Worthingtons decided to abide by her wishes and released the guard from their employ."

"Does Pandora know all of this?"

"Not unless Pepper told her at some point," Salinger informed me. "As far as the Worthingtons know, when she became Pepper, she left Stella Worthington behind."

"We need to tell Pandora. She might be able to help us figure this whole thing out."

"So far, no one knows that the woman who died isn't Ms. Worthington and her parents would like to keep it that way."

"Why?"

"Like I said, the Worthingtons want to conduct their own search for their daughter without interference from law enforcement. They believe they know how to handle this better than I would."

I realized they could be right about that. Salinger was a small-town sheriff. What did he know about hostage negotiation, if Pepper was indeed being held against her will? Of course, at this point we didn't really know that. In fact, we really didn't know much of anything at all.

"Can the Worthingtons request that you not investigate?" I asked.

"I suppose right now I don't have cause to do so. No one has filed a missing persons report and we haven't had a ransom demand so, as far as we know, Ms. Worthington has simply gone off somewhere and failed to tell anyone of her intention. Without the Worthingtons' cooperation, I don't see what I can do."

"That doesn't make any sense."

"I know," Salinger agreed. "As much as I resent being told what I can and cannot investigate, from a legal standpoint my hands are tied. The Worthingtons are very rich and very powerful. It wouldn't serve me well to ignore their wishes, especially since I have nothing to go on."

"*Someone* died in that crash," I pointed out. I tried to remember if I'd noticed anything at all about the person driving Pandora's car. The individual had worn a full helmet and racing suit with long sleeves and gloves. As far as I could recall, there was nothing to indicate who might have been behind the wheel as the car pulled up to the starting line.

"Someone did die in the crash," Salinger acknowledged, "which is why I'm going to focus my energy on discovering the identity of the victim. If you're concerned about Pepper, I suggest you look for her on your own. Quietly." Salinger looked directly at me. "*Very* quietly," he emphasized.

"If you want me to try to find Pepper, I'll need to tell a few people," I insisted.

"Perhaps, if you use discretion. The Worthingtons won't be happy if they find out you're interfering in their business."

I looked toward the judges' booth, where Levi was already waiting. "I need to go. I'll give this some thought and call you when the derby is over. At the very least, I need to fill in Levi, Boomer, and Pandora. Maybe the four of us can figure this whole thing out without involving anyone else."

"Do you think you can trust Pandora and Boomer? They could be involved," Salinger warned me.

"They're not." I don't know why I was so certain of that, but I was.

"Stella Worthington is worth a lot of money. If she did reveal her true identity to Pandora, perhaps she's the one behind the kidnapping."

I thought back to Pandora's shock when I informed her that Pepper had died, and Boomer's depth of mourning when he thought the victim was Pandora. No, I decided, there was no way they were involved, and it I was going to find out who actually died in the fiery crash and where Pepper had been since yesterday morning, I was going to need their help.

The second round of the derby was as exciting as the first, ending with Boomer, Zelda, and Crusher as the finalists, which meant there would be three men and three women in the finals.

I looked at the clock on my phone. I'd promised Zak I'd attend the chili cook-off and classic car parade with him and Scooter, but I really needed to fill Levi, Pandora, and Boomer in on the latest development. After providing Zak with a shortened version of what had occurred, he agreed that I should meet with the others and catch up with him later in the evening. I was going to owe Zak big-time when this was over. It seemed like I always had to put the needs of others ahead of him, and I realized that I was going to have to address that issue at some point,

But not now. Not today. Today, I was going to figure out where Pepper was and who had died in the fire.

Chapter 11

"What do you mean, the woman who died in the crash wasn't Pepper?" Pandora screeched after I'd pulled her and Boomer to the side and told them that I needed to talk to them in private.

"Shh," I cautioned. "We're supposed to keep this quiet."

"So where is Pepper?" Pandora whispered.

I explained about the titanium screw and the kidnapping theory of Mr. and Mrs. Wentworth.

Pandora frowned. "Pepper is rich?"

"So I've been told."

"But she never has money," Pandora insisted. "That's why we usually share a room. Pepper can never afford her own. She had to work at a bar evenings after working for me all day to buy the car she entered into the derby. I think there's been some sort of a mistake."

"I think Pepper wanted to leave Stella Worthington behind when she left home to work for you. Based on what Salinger told me, it sounds like she didn't bring anything with her from her old life, including her checkbook and credit cards."

"If I had money, I'd take it," Boomer declared.

"Me too," Levi agreed.

"How about if we all meet at the boathouse in thirty minutes?" I suggested. "I have cold beer and a bag of stale peanuts."

"Stale peanuts?" Levi raised a brow.

"I haven't had time to go to the store since we've been back from our trip, but at least we can talk without having to worry about being overheard. Maybe we can come up with a way to figure this whole thing out."

Everyone agreed to the plan.

"And it's important that you don't mention any of this to anyone else. Salinger was *very* clear about that."

"What about Zak and Ellie?" Levi asked.

"I already filled Zak in," I said. "Ellie is busy with the food for the event, but if she comes around, we'll fill her in. But other than that, we all keep quiet until we decide on a plan."

By the time we'd all gathered at the boathouse, it was obvious Boomer and Pandora had discussed the situation in detail. After greeting the cats and tossing them each a couple of salmon treats, I joined Levi and the others on the deck. It was a warm afternoon, but luckily, the umbrella I'd set up to provide shade coupled with a cool breeze coming off the water provided a very comfortable environment in which to conduct our strategy session.

"Okay, let's begin with the question of who might have died when Pandora's car crashed if it wasn't Pepper," I said.

"Boomer and I have been discussing that, and the reality is that we have no idea who might be lying in the morgue," Pandora started. "We personally have seen everyone who might have had access to my keys since the accident. It makes no sense."

"Maybe the driver didn't have your keys," I suggested. "Maybe someone hot-wired the car and drove it to the race."

"Who would do that?" Pandora asked.

I had no idea.

"Maybe someone who had a financial stake in you winning the race," I tried, even though I knew my theory was lame.

"Financial stake?" Pandora asked.

"A sponsor, or maybe a bookie who had bet big that you'd win?"

Pandora frowned. "I guess it's possible, but it seems unlikely. Did they find keys in the wreck?"

"I didn't think to ask," I admitted. "Do you still have your keys?" I asked.

"They were on the dresser in my room and I didn't think to look," Pandora shared. "I'll check when we get back."

"I'll call Salinger and see if he knows," I offered.

I called Salinger while the others chatted. The keys—or at least what remained of the keys—had been recovered from the ignition.

"Whoever drove had the keys," I confirmed. "Might Pepper have given them to someone?"

"I guess she could have," Pandora acknowledged. "It makes sense that she would have enlisted someone else's help if she realized I wasn't going to make it to the race and she wasn't able to cover for me. Are you sure the person who died in the crash was female?"

"That's what Salinger said," I answered. "You're thinking of Dezee, who is also missing? I'd thought of him as well, but I'm pretty sure even our coroner can tell female bones from male."

Pandora rubbed her head with her right hand. I was pretty sure the situation was giving us *all* a headache.

"I have to be honest," Pandora finally spoke. "I'm a lot more concerned about Pepper's whereabouts than the identity of the body in the morgue at this point. We have effectively eliminated all the derby drivers as potential victims, but Pepper could be in real trouble."

"Yeah, and Dezee too," Boomer added.

"It does seem odd that they're both missing," Levi added. "Might they be somewhere together?"

Boomer and Pandora looked at each other.

"They did seem to have a thing going on," Pandora shared. "Pepper first introduced me to Dezee maybe seven or eight months ago. She said he was an old friend from school and asked if I could help him get started on the derby circuit. I gave him some advice and helped him find a car and he began traveling with Pepper and me. I'm pretty sure Pepper and Dezee were seeing each other between trips as well. Pepper never said as much, but I'd be willing to guess they're romantically involved. Still, it seems odd that they'd be gone this long if they were simply away on a lovers' tryst."

"Does Pepper have any other friends she might have gone to see?" I asked Pandora.

"Not that I know of."

"And Dezee?"

"Not that he's ever mentioned."

I took a sip of my beer as I pondered the possibilities. On one hand, it sort of felt like things were all tied together in some way. On the other, I really couldn't see how a spiked drink, a car tampering, and two missing people who didn't appear to be together could be related at all.

"Do you know whether Salinger tried to track the cell phone of either missing person?" Levi asked.

"He says that neither phone is giving off a signal," I verified.

"They have to be somewhere together," Pandora decided. "It's the only thing that even remotely makes sense."

"What possible reason could kidnappers have for taking Dezee?" Boomer asked.

"We didn't know that Pepper was rich, but she did say she knew Dezee from school, so maybe he's rich too and, like Pepper, is hiding his wealth for some reason."

It occurred to me that Pandora had a point. I suspected that Stella Worthington attended an exclusive private school, so if she knew Dezee from there, it seemed likely that he came from money as well. Maybe someone had seen an opportunity to snag two heirs for the effort of one and took it. If so, that explained where our missing drivers were, but not who died in the crash or tampered with the car.

"There are just too many pieces to make sense of this whole thing." Boomer groaned.

"Here's what we know," Levi began. "Someone tampered with Pandora's car, with the intention, we can assume, either of killing her or whoever was driving the car at the time of the race. Pandora was drugged the night before the race. That may or may not be related to the tampering. We have a dead body in the morgue with no identity and two missing persons who seem to have vanished without a trace. Neither, it seems, can be the victim."

"Sounds about right," I concluded.

"So where do we even start?" Boomer asked, leaning back in his chair.

"We start with what we know," I decided. "Someone who was partying with Boomer and Pandora on Wednesday night drugged Pandora. That gives us a limited pool of suspects. According to notes I'd previously made, there were eight people in attendance that evening: Boomer, Pandora, Pepper, Dezee, Jugs, Masher, Rizo, and Big Boy Branson. We can eliminate the two of you, and we don't have a way to interview Pepper or Dezee at this point, but I'm going to suggest that you speak to the others and extract a confession one way or another."

"I'm on it," Boomer stated.

I turned to Pandora. "You stated that on the night in question, Dezee walked you back to your room and Pepper put you to bed. It seems likely that the two might have met up after that point, especially if, as you suspect, the two are lovers. Someone could have seen something. Why don't you talk to everyone and see if they remember seeing the pair after Dezee dropped you off? Did Dezee have his own room?"

"No. He was sharing with Crusher," Boomer answered.

"But Crusher wasn't at the party in your room?" I verified.

"No, but neither was Zelda, so I'm thinking they were hooking up."

"Okay, so the room might have been unoccupied and Dezee and Pepper might have gone back there to be alone. I think one of you should talk to Crusher and have a look around the room to see if you can find anything that might give us a clue as to whether

Pepper and Dezee were in the room, and where they might have gone after they left."

"Okay," Boomer and Pandora agreed.

"I'm going to call Zak to see if he'll come home to do a Web search for us. I want to know everything there is to know about Stella Worthington. Do we know Dezee's real name?"

Pandora and Boomer looked at each other and shrugged.

"I'll check with Willa. I'm pretty sure the contestants must have drivers' licenses on file in order to participate in the parade. Maybe I can track down his family to see if they've heard from him. Call me if you find anything significant; otherwise let's all meet up in the morning to plan our next move."

I called Zak, who left Scooter with Ellie before meeting Levi and me at his house. A very enthusiastic Charlie greeted me as I walked through the front door. Charlie had been having fun with Zak, Scooter, and Bella the past couple of days, but I knew he missed me as well. The two of us actually spend very little time apart. The fact that he is a certified therapy dog allows me to take him pretty much everywhere I go, so we aren't used to spending significant stretches away from each other.

"I've got a couple of desktops all set up to go," Zak informed me after kissing me hello. "The search engine is a lot faster than anything I have on any of my laptops. I figure if we find anything you want to look at, I can keep searching while you read. Where do we start?"

"Let's start with Pepper. According to Salinger, she's actually heiress Stella Worthington of the Worthington Aeronautics family."

Zak typed in a command and several photos popped up. It was definitely her. I looked at the photos while Levi checked the score of the baseball game on his phone. I knew he cared about what happened to Pepper and Dezee, but he tended to have a short attention span when it came to computer work.

There were dozens if not hundreds of photos of Pepper: competing in equestrian competitions, attending benefits, and accompanying her parents to exotic locations all over the world. According to the accompanying news articles, she was the only child of the wealthy couple and therefore the sole heir to a vast fortune.

I scanned through a sampling of photos of her as a child. She was beautiful, with a huge smile and dancing eyes. Based on the photos I'd accessed, it looked like she'd been happy, with a fabulous childhood, but as she got older, her enthusiastic smile morphed into a frown and the light in her eyes was replaced with a look of despair. I had to wonder what had occurred to bring on such a big change.

"Here's an article about when she fell and dislocated her shoulder," I said, bringing to an end any doubts I might have had as to her parents' insistence that the body in the morgue couldn't be their daughter.

I studied a photo of Pepper's thirteenth birthday. The smile was still firmly in place, so whatever occurred in her life to cause her to leave everything behind most likely had occurred after that point.

"Wow, she was raised like royalty," I commented as I continued to look through the photos. "She went to the best schools, had important friends, and traveled the world."

"Why would anyone leave that behind?" Levi wondered.

"I suppose that the saying that money can't buy happiness is probably true."

I looked at Zak, who just winked at me. I was pretty sure I knew what brought him happiness and it wasn't money.

"Look at this." I sat back so that Zak and Levi could see the photo I was looking at. "Here's a photo of Pepper at her Sweet Sixteen party. Do you see that girl standing next to her?"

"Yeah. So?" Levi asked.

"It says her name is Isabelle Stanford, but she looks familiar to me."

Levi frowned. "Maybe she has one of those faces that looks like someone else."

"Maybe."

I continued to look through the photos until I found a photo of Pepper's graduation from a very exclusive girls' school. Isabelle was standing off to the side and behind her rather than next to her, as in several of the other photos. Neither girl was smiling. The series of photos I studied, which had to have been taken between Stella's sixteenth birthday and her high school graduation, featured several girls who were included in all of the photos. I'm not sure why I focused in on Isabelle rather than the other girls who must have been close to Pepper when she was growing up. The more I stared at Isabelle, the more certain I was that I'd seen her somewhere before.

Could she have attended one of the events I'd been to this week? It made sense that she might, if she was friends with Pepper.

I found a couple of other photos after graduation, all of which featured an unsmiling Pepper. Isabelle seemed to have disappeared after graduation. At least she was no longer part of the crowd surrounding Pepper. Perhaps they'd had a falling-out? Could the reason for the falling-out be the catalyst that had caused Pepper's beautiful smile to fade?

"Do we know when Pepper joined up with Pandora?" I asked.

"Pandora said something about three years," Levi answered.

"And do we know how old she is?"

"According to her driver's license, she's twenty-two," Zak informed me.

"So if we assume she graduated high school at eighteen and joined the divas three years ago, she must have joined them about a year after she graduated high school, which is about the time the photos of her stopped."

"So?" Levi asked.

Yeah, so? I realized the fact that I was beginning to establish a timeline and a possible motive for Pepper leaving her family didn't help us find her. It also didn't help us identify the body in the morgue or figure out who drugged Pandora or rigged her car. I'd tried to get Willa on the phone to ask about Dezee's driver's license in an attempt to learn his real name, but she hadn't answered or returned my calls. I realized she was busy with the events in town.

"Anyone want to go to the chili cook-off?" I asked.

Chapter 12

By the time we returned to town, the walkways along Main Street were packed with spectators waiting to cheer on the classic cars as they cruised by to the music of the fifties and sixties. Levi and I saved a place in front of Rosie's Café while Zak went to fetch Scooter from Ellie. We'd decided to leave the dogs at home because of the crowds that were expected to descend on our little town by the time the park lit up with the thousands of twinkle lights volunteers had strung onto every tree they could reach.

"You made it." Mom kissed me and then handed Harper over to me as she and my dad squeezed in beside us.

"Couldn't miss the parade." I kissed Harper on the cheek. She was dressed in an adorable pink skirt with a white poodle stitched on the front and a white cardigan sweater over a pink onesie. Ankle socks and white leather shoes rounded out the outfit. I was certain there had never been a cuter baby in the history of all babies anywhere.

"Harper looks adorable. Where did you find this outfit?"

"From a retro baby store online," Mom answered. "I thought you were going to dress up?"

"Long day, no time or energy," I answered. "You guys look cute."

Mom had on lime green capris and a bright yellow top and my dad was wearing blue jeans with the cuffs rolled up and a white T-shirt with the sleeves folded over what I suspected was a deck of cards because he didn't smoke. He also wore white tube socks with black dress shoes, giving him a retro if not dorky look. I loved it.

"Thanks," Mom answered. "I just love the bright colors of the sixties, and your dad looks so handsome in his Levi's. Where's Zak?"

"He went to get Scooter, who's been hanging out with Ellie for the past couple of hours. He should be here any minute. Are you going to the chili cook-off?"

"Wouldn't miss it," Mom answered. "I had lunch with Ava from our birthing class last week, and she told me that she was entering a vegetarian black bean version that sounds delicious."

"How is Jasmine doing?"

Jasmine is Ava's baby, who's about three weeks older than Harper. It seemed like Mom and Ava were developing a close friendship, even though Ava was at least ten years younger than her. I was happy to see Mom putting down roots. In my own mind, with every friend she made or group she joined, she was just a bit less likely to pack up and leave, as she had so many times before.

"She's doing really well, considering the rough start she had."

Jasmine had been born six weeks premature, weighing less than five pounds.

"She's almost caught up to Harper in terms of weight. Ava has decided that she feels secure enough to leave her for a few hours a week, so we hired a friend of Hazel's to watch the girls and have started volunteering at the library two afternoons a week during the children's reading hour. I didn't think I'd like spending *that* much time with *that* many kids, but Ava persuaded me to give it a try and I love it."

"That's wonderful." I smiled. "Are you still doing the spin class on Tuesday and Thursday evenings?"

"As often as I can. I think I'm pretty close to talking Ava into doing it with me, now that her husband got his hours switched from swing to days and is home in the evenings to watch Jasmine. By the way, how did the derby go?"

"Surprisingly well, considering. Pandora, Boomer, Jaqui, Masher, Zelda, and Crusher are all in the finals. It should be a really good contest."

"Heard any more about the accident?" Dad joined the conversation.

"Some, but I really can't discuss it right now. Maybe I can stop by the house tomorrow, where we can talk in private?"

"Come for breakfast," Mom invited.

"I'd love to, but I have a seven a.m. meeting. Dad does as well."

"Oh, that's right. I'd forgotten. Just come by whenever you can get away."

I turned to watch the long row of cars slowly drive by. There were a variety of makes and models in a rainbow of colors. Most of the cars originally had been manufactured in the sixties and seventies, but there were several from the fifties and a few from the thirties and forties. My favorites were the large sedans from the fifties and sixties.

"Now there's a car with solid bones." Dad whistled as a '57 Chevy Bel Air Sport Sedan, red with a white top, slowly drove by. The car had been meticulously restored and maintained.

"It really is a beautiful car," I commented. "I bet it cost a pretty penny to restore."

"And worth every penny. They don't make them like that anymore. Your pappy had one just like that when I was a kid. He got it new and kept it until after I'd graduated high school and left home."

"What happened to it?" I asked.

"He sold it to pay for the European vacation he took your grandma on for their anniversary. He said it was her dream, and he wanted to be sure she was able to fulfill it before they were both too old to enjoy it."

I looked around as a stepside truck from the mid-fifties rolled by.

"Where is Pappy anyway? I thought he might come with you."

"Nick entered the chili contest and Pappy is helping him," Dad informed me. "They're doing a version with shredded beef and just a bit of a kick. I had a small taste earlier and it was fantastic."

If my dad said it had "a bit of a kick," that most likely meant it was so hot it was inedible to most. Dad and I like our chili spicy.

"I can't wait to try it." The chili cook-off was my dad's baby, so I asked him how it was going.

"Good," he said. "We have eight entrants. The judging has already taken place, although the winner won't be announced until later. The chili is available for purchase if you're hungry. All the proceeds go to the library this year."

"Actually, I'm starving."

I waved at Zak, who was pushing his way through the crowd with Scooter on his shoulders. Scooter had the biggest smile I'd ever seen. He was obviously enjoying his time with Zak, and based on Zak's own grin, I'd say he was having a wonderful time as well.

"Zak bought me some cotton candy," Scooter told me.

"Have you had dinner yet?"

"We'll get some after the parade," Zak said.

"He's going to spoil his dinner with all that sugar," I predicted.

Zak shrugged. "It's a special occasion."

"He's going to be high as a kite. We'll never get him to bed."

"He's fine," Zak assured me. "A little sugar never hurt anyone."

Dad laughed out loud. "You guys sound like an old married couple."

I smiled. I guess we did.

After the parade, we headed over to the chili cook-off. There were so many wonderful options to choose from, I had no idea where to start. I decided to take just a bite of each offering in the hope of trying them all. The chili Pappy and Nick had prepared was delicious—and hot—but I think my favorite was the white bean with chicken and green chilies that Rosie had entered.

"Mom and I are going to take Harper home," Dad informed me after we'd eaten and Nick had been declared the winner of the contest. "I'll see you in the morning." He kissed me on the cheek.

"Okay, see you then." I waved as they headed toward the parking lot.

"I should get Scooter home as well," Zak added. "Charlie is still at my house. Do you want to come by after you're done here, or should I drop him off at your place?"

"I'll come by. We never did get a chance to talk last night. I shouldn't be too late, although I should head over to the snack shack and offer to help clean up."

"Okay." Zak kissed me. "I'll be waiting."

I looked around for Levi, who had wandered off while I was having dinner with my family. Ellie should be just about done at the snack bar, so I headed in that direction. I still hoped to track Willa down to see if she knew Dezee's real name. I wasn't sure how that could help us, but at this point any answer to even a small part of the very confusing puzzle we were dealing with had to be of some help.

I hadn't seen Pandora or Boomer all evening. I supposed they might have decided that an early night was in order, given the stress of the past few days. I wasn't surprised that Pandora hadn't participated in the parade since her car had been crushed beyond recognition, but I was a little surprised that Boomer hadn't shown up to showcase his Mustang Mach 1.

I'd been watching to see if Dezee showed up at the last minute to take part in the event, but I hadn't seen him, and the other participants I'd surveyed had reported that they hadn't seen him since before the accident.

"Need any help?" I asked Ellie and Tawny, who were in the process of closing up the snack shack for the night.

"I think we're about done," Ellie informed me. "It was a good day, but I can't remember the last time I was this exhausted."

"Were you here all day?" I asked.

"Almost. We did get a few breaks, but we're going to have to make certain to line up a larger volunteer force next year."

"Tell me about it." Tawny yawned. She pulled her long blond ponytail around to the front of her face and gave it a sniff. "I smell like hamburger grease. I'm probably going to have to lather, rinse, and repeat about a hundred times to get the smell out."

"You might as well just wait until after we close up on Sunday to go to that much trouble," I suggested. "I'm betting tomorrow is going to be a long day for all of us."

Ellie groaned.

"How about a beer? My treat," I offered.

Tawny declined. "I need to get home to my kids."

"I'm in." Ellie bent from side to side to relieve the kinks in her back. "I haven't been able to leave this exact spot for most of the day. You can catch me up."

She grabbed her backpack and, after promising Tawny that she'd be at the 7 a.m. meeting Willa had requested, looped her arm through mine as we headed to the beer garden that had been set up near the bandstand, where a band from out of the area was playing music from the fifties and sixties.

"How did the derby go?" Ellie asked.

I filled her in on the contestants and the eight who had made it to the finals.

"I'm surprised Pandora participated after what happened with Pepper. I know they were close."

As she spoke, I realized Ellie still believed that Pepper was the victim in the crash yesterday morning.

"Let's grab our beer and find a seat. I have news that's going to blow you away."

I spent the next half hour bringing Ellie up to date on *all* the events of the day.

"Wow, it looks like you really have yourself a mystery," Ellie stated when I had finished my tale. "I'm sorry I missed everything."

"I'm not sure how to even approach this whole thing. The hardest part is that after the awards ceremony on Sunday, everyone involved is going to leave, so solving the mystery is going to be close to impossible. I just keep hoping we can find some small piece of evidence that ties everything together."

"I can snoop around while I'm working the snack bar," Ellie offered.

"You'll need to be careful. Remember, most people don't know that Pepper wasn't the victim in the crash and Salinger wants to keep it that way. I probably shouldn't have told you, but best friends don't keep secrets."

"I should hope not," Ellie agreed.

"How did your lunch with Jeremy go?" I wondered.

Ellie bit her lip as she appeared to be considering her answer.

"It went fine," she eventually said. "Jeremy is such a nice guy, and he really did have some good insights. He's going to let me visit with Morgan once the weekend is over and I'm not so busy. He thinks that if I'm going to continue with my campaign to have a baby, I should spend some time with one. I think his intention is sweet, and I would love to have a chance to play with Morgan, but I've babysat a *lot* of babies in my life and I really feel I know what I'm getting into. Still, when Jeremy offered to let me spend time with his adorable little angel, I wasn't going to say no."

"Morgan *is* a sweetie. And I'm sure helping Jeremy with Morgan will help him out as well."

"Yeah, I figured. So about picking me a date . . ."

I groaned. I'd hoped Ellie had forgotten all about that.

"I've narrowed the five down to three. I left my laptop in my car, but maybe you can take a look tomorrow?"

"Of course I will. I'm sorry I forgot about it. It looks like Willa is coming this way. I need to talk to her, and then I should get going. See you in the morning?"

"I'll be there," Ellie said.

I jogged across the park to catch up with Willa before she left for the day. It had been a long one for everyone on the committee, and I was sure she was as exhausted as I was.

"Zoe, how did everything go?" Willa asked.

"As well as can be expected given the circumstances," I answered. "I'm looking into a few things for Salinger and I wondered if you knew Dezee's real name. He's still missing."

"I have the files in my car if you want to walk over to the parking lot with me."

I took one of the two large bags Willa was carrying and walked with her toward her car.

"It seems like we had a good turn out," I said.

She nodded. "I'm pretty sure we had record-breaking numbers. I'm anxious to tally everything up, but I'm guessing we did *very* well today. How was the derby?"

I filled Willa in.

"The drivers who are left should draw a good crowd tomorrow."

I agreed.

Willa set her bag on the ground in order to unlock her car doors. I put both bags on the backseat while she looked through her files on the passenger side of the front.

"According to this paperwork, Dezee's real name is Izick Stanford."

Izick Stanford. As in Isabelle Stanford? Perhaps a brother?

Chapter 13

Saturday, July 12

Although I'd decided to spend the night at my boathouse in order to hang out with Marlow and Spade, I'd arranged with Zak to come by after I'd attended the 7 a.m. meeting and helped with the setup for the day's events. By the time I'd gotten to Zak's the previous evening, I'd realized I was much too tired and distracted to have the talk we kept promising each other we'd have, so I'd collected Charlie and headed home.

Luckily, Willa had recruited extra help from community members not on the committee, so the setup went quickly and I was able to meet with Zak by nine.

"Coffee is on." Zak kissed me as I walked in the door with Charlie on my heels. Bella ran up to greet us, and the two dogs headed out the back to frolic and play.

"Where's Scooter?" I asked.

"Sleeping. He had a bit of a rough night. I guess you were right about the sugar."

I smiled.

"Would you like some breakfast?" Zak asked. "I made boysenberry muffins this morning with the last of the berries I picked up at the farmers market."

"When did you have time to go to the farmers market? You've only been home a couple of days and you've had Scooter the entire time."

"I ran over before the beach yesterday. I can make you some eggs to go with the muffins if you'd like, or I have sausage from the butcher."

"The muffins are fine."

Sometimes when I'm with Zak I feel like a total slacker. The man seems to be able to juggle a hundred different things at once without breaking a sweat. He actually got up and made muffins? I hadn't even had time to go to the store to buy milk since we'd been back from our trip. If we were meeting at my boathouse, we'd be dining on frozen pizza or canned vegetables.

"So do you want to talk or just eat?" Zak asked.

I knew we should talk about the thing we'd been avoiding for almost a week now, but what I really wanted to do was ask for Zak's help with the murder investigation. "I hate to even ask," I hedged.

"You want to continue with our research," Zak guessed.

"Hate me?" I tried for a pathetic face.

Zak kissed my nose before picking up his coffee and heading to his office, where his desktop computers were set up.

"Where do you want to start?" he asked once he'd logged on.

"I'd like to start off by finding out whether Isabelle Stanford and Izick Stanford are related," I answered. "Even if they aren't, I'm not certain this bit of knowledge is relevant to the mystery we're faced with, but somehow I feel like this piece of information might be important."

"Spelling?" Zak asked.

I repeated what had been on Dezee's driver's license.

Zak began typing while I sipped my coffee. I was sorry Scooter had had a bad night, but I was happy we could work in peace and quiet. Scooter was nice enough, but he had the energy level of ten kids put together. I don't know how his grandparents kept up with him. I watched Zak as he worked. He was good with the boy. Scooter respected Zak in a way he did very few adults; a stern look was usually enough to get him to settle down and take care of what needed to be done. He was going to make some lucky kid a great dad.

"That's odd." Zak frowned at the screen. "I can't find a driver's license for an Izick Stanford. Which state was the license from?"

I thought about it. "Massachusetts."

Zak typed some more while I pulled up the photos from Pepper's past that we'd been looking at on the other computer. I tried to imagine what could have happened to cause Stella to leave behind such a glamorous life to follow Pandora around the country from one dive motel to the next. Not that the Ashton Falls Motor Inn was a dive motel, but it certainly wasn't the Ritz. Based on the photos I'd found, Stella Worthington had never experienced anything other than five star or first class in her life until she'd run away and become Pepper.

"I have a driver's license for Isabelle Stanford from Massachusetts, but nothing for Izick."

"Maybe I got the state wrong. Hang on; I'll call Willa."

I checked with Willa while Zak continued to search through the public records. Willa confirmed that the license had been issued by the state of Massachusetts and that the photo on the license matched the driver known as Dezee.

"According to what I can find based on the public records available, Isabelle Stanford is twenty-nine years old."

"Twenty-nine? But she went to school with Pepper, who is only twenty-two. It must not be the same person."

Zak pulled up her photo. I frowned. It *looked* like the same person. Based on the photos I'd found of Pepper in high school, Isabelle first showed up shortly before Pepper's sixteenth birthday. She continued to appear in photos of Pepper at school and attending social events until after Pepper graduated when she was eighteen. Why would a woman who had to be in her mid-twenties be attending an all-girls' high school? Unless she was the bodyguard Pepper's parents had hired, masquerading as an ordinary high school student . . .

"Isabelle must be—" I started.

"The bodyguard," Zak finished.

"So how does Izick tie into all of this?" I wondered.

"Maybe he doesn't," Zak suggested. "According to everything I can find, Isabelle was an only child who was raised by her father after her mother died when she was six. Her father owned a martial arts school, which probably explains how Isabelle was qualified to be a bodyguard. Even though she was in her twenties when she attended the same high school as Stella Worthington, she looked much younger than her age, so I imagine she had no problem fitting in. You mentioned that Stella's parents fired the bodyguard at Stella's request. What if Stella didn't know that Isabelle was hired to keep an eye on her, then felt betrayed by her best friend when she found out?"

"I had that exact same thought yesterday. It's like we have the same brain."

"Trust me, we don't have the same brain. You'd probably slug me right now if you could read my thoughts," Zak teased.

"Why?"

Zak wiggled his eyebrows at me.

"You are such a pervert. Now focus."

"Oh, I'm focused."

"On Isabelle and Izick," I clarified.

Zak stared at the screen and frowned. "Even if Izick and Isabelle aren't related, there should still be a record of Izick unless his license is a fake."

"Maybe it is a fake." That made as much sense as anything.

Zak continued to type. I watched his face as he worked. The slight furrow between his brows was oh so sexy, as was the way he chewed on his bottom lip with his perfectly white teeth. Maybe we should take a break. Scooter was still sleeping, and who knew when we'd have time to . . .

"I think I found something," Zak announced, interrupting my fantasy. "Isabelle Stanford let her driver's license lapse shortly after she would have been fired from her bodyguard job. She didn't renew it in any other state as far as I can tell. I did, however, find a credit card in her name. The last charge showing up was for five nights at the Ashton Falls Motor Inn."

"So Isabelle paid for Izick to stay here. They *must* be related. Maybe they're cousins, if they aren't siblings. Maybe Isabelle wanted Izick to spy on Pepper. Maybe he even drugged Pandora and arranged for the car to crash, figuring that Pepper would fill in for her best friend and he could get revenge for what Pepper did to Isabelle. Not that killing someone is equitable revenge for getting someone you cared about fired from your job," I rambled on.

Zak continued to frown at the computer screen as he appeared to be analyzing something he was reading. "I think it's more than that," he concluded. "I think Izick Stanford and Isabelle Stanford are the same person."

"The same person?"

Of course. We'd assumed all along that one of the derby drivers showed up to cover for Pandora, but Dezee was the only driver who was missing other than Pepper, and since the victim was female, we figured it had to be Pepper. We never suspected that the victim was Dezee because we all believed he was male. But if Dezee was really Isabelle in disguise . . .

"Why?" I asked. "Why would Isabelle masquerade as a guy? And if Dezee is a female and Pepper and Dezee are involved, then Pepper must know who Dezee really is. The whole thing makes no sense."

"I don't know why Isabelle did what she did," Zak said, "but we really should fill in Salinger at this point."

"So where does this leave us?" I asked Salinger after he'd informed me that based on a cursory investigation of the badly burned corpse, the two could be the same person.

"Isabelle Stanford's next of kin will be notified that she was killed in the accident, effectively closing the case."

"Closing the case?" I asked. "We still don't know for certain that the body is Isabelle, and we don't know who tampered with the car, where Pepper is, who drugged Pandora, or why Isabelle was masquerading as a man in the first place."

"It's not against the law to present oneself as a man and therefore not a police matter," Salinger informed me. "As for Ms. Worthington, her parents have informed me that they have heard from the kidnapper and are arranging to meet the ransom demand. They were very clear that they don't want the police involved."

"Okay then, who drugged Pandora?" I asked.

"We don't have any proof that she was drugged," Salinger said. "Drugs were found in her system, but for all we know, she could have ingested the sedatives herself."

"Why would she do that?"

I was beginning to feel desperate. The sheriff, in a typical Salinger move, was about to sweep things under the rug in order to avoid a controversy.

"People take drugs all the time," he pointed out. "Maybe Pandora was so wasted that she forgot she had taken them, or maybe she did remember but was covering her own tracks after a horrible accident that took someone's life while they were operating her car."

Salinger had a point, but I still thought he was wrong. His explanation was *much* too easy.

"Okay, let's discuss the car," I decided. "Someone tampered with the car. Surely you still need to investigate *that*."

"My guys tell me the brake line could have severed on its own if the car hadn't been properly maintained. The timing of the leak reaching a critical point was unfortunate, but it doesn't necessarily prove intent."

"You've got to be freaking kidding me. You're really closing the book on *all* of this?"

I could feel my blood begin to boil as Salinger sat back in his chair with a look of disinterest on his face.

"I'm afraid I *am* going to close the book on all of this, and you should too. You have a derby to run and a sock hop to attend. Don't waste your time chasing after a conspiracy theory that simply won't lead anywhere. Now, if you'll excuse me, I have a phone call to make."

Salinger picked up the phone and, with that, I was affectively dismissed.

After I left Salinger's office, I called Zak, who had stayed behind with Scooter and the dogs, and asked if he had time to chat. Returning to the festivities until I'd had time to let off some steam was completely unthinkable. I could have called Levi, and he would have come in an instant, but sometimes I just need Zak. He has a way of calming me that no one else ever has.

Luckily, Scooter was quite contently watching cartoons with the dogs after his big adventure the previous day. Zak and I retired to his office, where we could talk but still keep an eye on the small tornado who still had a tendency to kick up a gust every now and then. Zak sat down in his desk chair while I lay down on the sofa. I stared at the ceiling as I told Zak everything Salinger had told me.

"Salinger is taking the easy way out," Zak responded after I had finished my tale. "It's what he always does."

"So what are we going to do? Walk away like he wants us to?"

"Is there a reason we shouldn't?"

I sat up. "Of course there's a reason we shouldn't. Dezee is dead and we don't know why. Pandora was drugged and we don't know by whom. Someone tampered with Pandora's car and we don't know who the intended victim was. Assuming it wasn't Dezee, it's possible whoever cut the brake lines will try again. And, finally, we don't *really* know that Pepper is okay. There must be a way to put the pieces together and figure out what really happened."

Zak hesitated. I knew that look. He had an idea he wasn't sure was a good idea, but he knew I'd jump all over it, so he was hesitating to mention it.

"Too late. I recognize that look. What are you thinking?"

"Maybe we can let Dezee and Pepper tell us what happened," he suggested.

"Dezee is dead and Pepper is who knows where. How can they tell us anything?" I complained.

"If we decide that it's a good idea to do so—and I'm not saying that it is—" Zak qualified, "I can probably hack into Dezee's and Pepper's e-mail and texts. I suppose that might tell us something we don't already know."

I smiled. "That's perfect. Why the hesitation?"

"Looking at someone's private texts and e-mails is like reading a diary. It's very invasive and something I really never do. In this case, however, I think it may be the only way to get the answers we need."

"Let's do it," I said. "How do we start?"

"Do we have access to either Dezee's or Pepper's phones or laptops?" Zak asked.

"I'll call Pandora and find out."

An hour later, we had Pepper's laptop. Neither phone could be found.

"This feels so weird," Pandora commented. Both she and Boomer had decided to stay while Zak did his thing. "It really makes me rethink the content of the e-mails and texts I send."

"Tell me about it," Boomer said. "Is there any way to permanently erase that type of thing?"

"Yeah, if you know how," Zak answered.

"The fact that Dezee was a chick is really freaking me out," Boomer shared. "I keep thinking back to all the times I paraded around naked in front of him."

"So?" Pandora teased. "Everyone knows you like to strut your stuff."

Boomer threw a pillow at her.

"The fact that Dezee was really a chick is strange, but what I'm most worried about is Pepper," Pandora said. "I know Salinger said her parents have it handled, but to be honest, I don't really trust them."

"Do you know why she left? She gave up a lot," I pointed out.

"Pepper never let on for one minute that she was loaded, but she did say a few things about why she never wanted to go home for the holidays. It seems she was in love and her parents didn't approve of her relationship, so as soon as she could, she bailed."

"Did she ever hook up with the guy she left her family for?" I wondered.

"I never saw her with a guy," Pandora answered.

"Or maybe she did," Zak interrupted. "I found Pepper's diary."

We all looked at Zak expectantly.

"I'm not going to read any of this to you, or share more details than I have to, but here's what I think is relevant," he began. "Pepper did leave her home and her family over an argument she had with her parents regarding a love affair. The affair wasn't with a guy, however."

"Isabelle," I realized. "Stella fell in love with the older woman her parents hired to protect her. When they found out, they fired Isabelle and refused to let Stella see her, and she ran away so they could be together. It's so romantic."

"Okay, so why was Isabelle parading around as a guy?" Boomer asked.

"And why was Dezee in my car and where is Pepper?" Pandora asked.

Chapter 14

We decided that Zak would keep digging for clues while Boomer, Pandora, Levi, and I went to the derby finals. We figured it was best if we presented a front of business as usual in case whoever was holding Pepper or trying to kill Pandora was watching. What it came down to, we thought, was that there had to be someone on the inside orchestrating the whole thing. Someone with access to the alcohol Pandora drank as well as the cars. Of course, there could be more than one person involved. One partner could have been drugging Pandora while the other was slicing into the brake lines. Zak suggested that we trust no one until we figured the whole thing out.

The derby had been hyped as the derby to end all derbies once the finalists were announced. The group involved would likely provide a show that was all that and more. The crowd today was even bigger than it had been for the preliminary rounds. As it had been all week, the sun was beating down on the crowd, making me think that perhaps an evening event would have worked out better this year. The bleachers at the fairgrounds in Bryton Lake that we normally used were covered, providing shade for most of the day, while the pasture provided no protection from the sun at all.

The crowd roared as Levi announced each finalist. The fact that there were three men against three women added an element of team play as the girls lined up against the guys. As the moments ticked down to the official start, the noise level generated by the enthusiastic crowd created a vibration in the air surrounding the fenced-in pasture that seemed to escalate with each passing second.

The fact that someone had already died that weekend in a fiery crash brought the element of danger to the forefront of everyone's mind, which, in my opinion, created a sort of mania as the crowd wondered whether further injuries would result from what could be a violent contest.

In the opening moments, there were groans as Pandora, Jaqui, and Zelda ganged up on Crusher simultaneously, hitting him from all sides. I suspected that the sexes might work together, at least in the opening minutes, but it seemed clear to me that the three women had discussed exactly what to do before the event even began.

With Crusher out of the way, it was three girls to two guys. I was curious to see whether the remaining guys would work together against the girls now, but it seemed that once the opening volley had been played out, everyone was fighting to gain his own territory.

The next to become disabled was Zelda, once again evening out the playing field as Boomer skillfully took out one of her tires. Pandora took out Masher at just about the same time Jaqui had tried for Boomer, only to have her strategy backfire as Boomer whipped around and hit her head-on.

By the time the second hand on the clock had made a full rotation five times, the field was down to Pandora and Boomer. I was curious to see how that rivalry would play out. Would Boomer play the gentleman and let Pandora take the win?

Apparently not.

The crowd roared as the two opponents rammed each other time and time again, until neither vehicle resembled much of a car at all. The final moments of the event were almost too painful to watch as the two cars crawled along, trying to deliver that one critical wallop.

"What happens if they both just stop running?" Levi asked.

"I don't know," I whispered back. "Maybe it would be considered a tie."

"A tie would be anticlimactic, but at this point I don't see how either car is continuing on."

"They both seem really determined."

We watched as Pandora crept forward on three tires while Boomer jockeyed to get into position in spite of the fact that smoke was pouring from the hood of his car. Everyone held their breath as Pandora delivered the final death blow and once again emerged the victor. A roar went up as Boomer jumped out of his car and helped Pandora from hers. The arrival of a 747 wouldn't have been heard as the crowd went wild, with Boomer pulling Pandora into his arms and engaging her in a lip-lock to rival all lip-locks. The crowd cheered and chanted as both cars smoked in the background.

By the time the crowd had dissipated and Levi and I were free to leave, I felt like all the life had been drained from my limbs. Who knew that watching cars smash into one another could be such an emotionally draining experience?

When I got to Zak's, he was in the pool with Scooter. The two were laughing and playing like a couple of pups, and I longed to do nothing more serious than join them. Boomer and Pandora had wandered off after the event, and I hadn't seen either of them since Boomer picked Pandora up and carried her into the crowd. I suspected that he had a car waiting to whisk her away for a romantic encounter after the foreplay the derby must have provided.

I headed upstairs and changed into a swimsuit I'd left in the dresser Zak had provided for the clothing I'd left there. At my place, he was lucky to get half a drawer. Of course, his place was huge while mine was small, so I tried to convince myself that the size of the space we provided for each other in no way represented the depth of our commitment.

"How'd it go?" Zak asked after I dove into the pool and swam up to his side.

"Pandora won, but it was a heck of a fight to the finish."

"And the others?"

"Off on their own. Did you find anything?"

"Not really."

I was glad we could focus on something else for a few hours.

"Watch me do a cannon ball," Scooter yelled as he jumped into the pool with his legs crossed, displacing quite a lot of water in the process.

"Way to go, champ. Your technique is improving," Zak complimented. "Are you getting hungry?"

"I'm starved."

"Why don't you go in and shower and change and I'll make us some dinner?" Zak suggested.

"'Kay," Scooter agreed.

I wrapped my arms around Zak's neck after Scooter headed indoors. I forced myself to relax as I forced my mind to release the tension from my body.

"I could sleep right here," I said as I closed my eyes and floated on the surface of the water.

"We have the sock hop," Zak reminded me.

"Oh yeah." I groaned. To be honest, I'd totally forgotten about it, in spite of the fact that we'd discussed it earlier in the day. Maybe I really was losing my mind.

"Why don't you head in and take a shower?" Zak said. "I'll take a quick shower in the guest bath and make dinner while you get ready."

"We could shower together," I suggested.

"As good as that sounds—" Zak kissed me on the lips. A long, deep kiss that left me wanting more. "Levi will be here to babysit in just over an hour."

I kissed Zak's neck. "We have an hour."

"Scooter will be down in less than ten minutes," Zak reminded me.

I moaned. Having kids definitely had a downside.

"Maybe we can skip the dance?"

"You promised several people, including your parents, that you'd be there," Zak reminded me.

"Yeah, I guess I did. Maybe we can leave early?" I hoped.

"Count on it."

Chapter 15

Entering the community center was like stepping back in time. The local five-and-dime must have been cleaned out of hair gel if the slicked-back do's of the men in attendance were any indication. Women in poodle skirts with hair the height of the Empire State Building were twisting and turning to the tunes of the fifties as men dressed in T-shirts and jeans attempted to display the perfect dip without dropping their dates unceremoniously on their heads.

"Wow, this place really looks great," I said to Hazel, who was clinging possessively to Pappy's arm. At first I wasn't sure how I felt about the fact that Pappy and Hazel were dating, but now that I'd had a chance to get used to seeing them together, I realized that they would be good for each other. My pappy had married my grandmother when they were very young, and as far as I knew, he'd hadn't dated anyone since, so I knew he was taking this relationship slowly.

"Gilda, Willa, and I spent the whole day making sure that everything was just right."

"Well, your hard work paid off. This place is really spectacular," I complimented. "And the band is the best one we've heard all weekend, although they've all been really great."

"We were just about to dance." Hazel glanced at Pappy, who was discussing classic cars with Zak. "I think Ellie might want to talk to you. She was looking for you earlier."

"She in the kitchen?" I asked.

"As always. That girl can cook, I'll give her that. You have to try the dip platter she set out. Each and every one of the choices is delicious, and if you prefer a lower-calorie option, she provided chopped veggies as well as several different types of chips and crackers. Not that you need to worry about calories. Oh, and do try the ahi appetizer. It's really the best I've ever had."

"I will," I promised. Zak had made us a huge dinner, so I really wasn't hungry, but maybe a small snack, just to be polite? "Have fun, you two."

"You too, darling." Pappy kissed me on the cheek before being pulled away by his very determined librarian.

"Zak, Zoe," Mom intercepted us. "I'm so glad you made it. I wasn't sure, with everything that's been going on."

"We figured we'd done all we could for the time being, and Levi volunteered to hang out with Scooter," I said.

"Levi is babysitting?" Mom sounded as shocked as I'd felt when he'd offered.

"Scooter isn't exactly a baby, and Levi said he wasn't planning to come here anyway. They ordered pizza and were neck and neck in a battle with the Cylons when we left."

"Cylons?"

"Video game," I informed her. "Who did you leave Harper with?"

"Jeremy. He offered to take her when he came for dinner the other night. I guess he's planning to stay home and watch videos with Jessica and Rosalie."

Jessica is a friend of Jeremy's and Rosalie is her daughter.

"It was good of him to offer."

"He's turned out to be such a nice young man."

I almost laughed out loud. My mom hadn't returned to the area until a year ago, so I figured she really had no idea what kind of man Jeremy was before he became a single father three months ago, but her assessment was right-on. Jeremy was a great guy who actually had been a little rough around the edges when I'd first met him.

"Did you talk to him about the music for the wedding?" I asked.

"We did, and he'll be perfect for our ceremony, won't he?" Mom asked Dad.

I could see that Dad and Zak hadn't been listening to our conversation, so he had no idea what Mom was referring to.

"The music for the wedding," I filled him in.

"Yes, Jeremy is very talented," Dad agreed. "I'm glad you suggested him."

"He brought his guitar and played some of the songs we were thinking about. The babies really seemed to like the music," Mom commented.

"I was sorry I missed the playdate."

"I don't know how much playing was going on. We laid them on a blanket and they seemed interested in each other. I'm betting they'll be good friends when they grow up. I thought I'd have Jeremy bring Morgan back over sometime soon, and I'll invite Ava and Jasmine as well. Ava and I discussed the idea of starting a mommies group—or, really, a mommies and daddies group—and Jeremy said he'd be happy to join in."

Suddenly, I found I was jealous that I didn't have a baby so I could join in the fun. My mom was putting down roots and making friends, which thrilled me, but somehow I felt excluded from this very important part of her life. Maybe Ellie's idea of having a baby wasn't so bad after all.

"I guess I should go find Ellie. Hazel said she was looking for me."

"I'm going to go say hi to Scott," Zak informed me. "I'll find you in a minute."

"I'll be in the kitchen."

I wondered if Scott was there alone. I hoped he'd invite Tiffany, but I didn't see her anywhere. Of course, she could just be in the ladies' room, and Scott didn't appear to be with anyone else.

As predicted, Ellie was standing over the stove, stirring something in a big pot.

"No blind date tonight?" I asked.

"I've been too busy the past few days to worry about dating," she informed me. "I did have a conversation with Kelly about my situation, and she has a friend she wants to introduce me to."

"A referral from a friend might yield better results than a computer dating service," I offered. "Kelly knows you pretty well, so she should have a good idea what you'd like and what you wouldn't."

"That's what I thought, so I agreed to give him a try. His name is Brady and he lives just down the hill in Bryton Lake. Kelly says he's really nice and very responsible and a total babe."

"Sounds promising."

"He owns his own consulting business and is thinking about relocating to Ashton Falls since he works from home and can live anywhere. She did say that the downside is that he travels for work a lot and has joint custody of three kids with his ex-wife."

"Messy divorce?" I asked.

"Sounds like it. That's the only thing Kelly told me that gave me pause. I really don't want to get in the middle of a couple who tends to do a lot of fighting. Still, I figured it was worth meeting him."

"How old are the kids?"

"Fourteen, eleven, and eight."

"So this guy must be in his thirties?"

"Kelly says he's thirty-eight, which I realize is quite a bit older than me, but maybe someone who's in his thirties will be more mature than someone in his twenties."

I couldn't believe I was about to say this, since I'd just told Ellie to try meeting a nice guy and not to be so focused on having a baby, but I felt it needed to be said, so I was going ahead. "Do you think a man who is thirty-eight with three children will be interested in having additional kids?" I asked.

Ellie frowned. "I hadn't thought of that."

"I know I said to concentrate on meeting a nice guy and not make having a baby the *most* important thing, but in this case I think the question is relevant. I'd hate to see you fall for this guy only to find out his view of babies is been there, done that. Just think about it."

"Yeah, I will. And thanks."

"So was there a reason you were looking for me, or did you just want to say hi?" I asked.

"Actually, I wanted to tell you what I'd heard about Jaqui. I was in the kitchen slicing fruit for the punch when I overheard two men talking. I didn't recognize either man, so I don't think they were involved in the derby, but it sounded like they were participating in the classic car show. Anyway, one of the men mentioned to the other that he had seen Jaqui messing around with Pandora's car the night before the race."

I frowned. I didn't know Jaqui well, but she seemed the type who *could* rig a car to crash. She certainly had the skill to do so, and based on her outward demeanor, she seemed to have the personality to do it as well.

"Did they say anything else?"

"No, that's all I heard. I don't even know for certain which car she was seen messing around with, but given the circumstances . . ."

It was true that Pandora had two cars, one for the derby and one to parade around in. Her derby car seemed to run fine, so chances were it was the car that crashed that Jaqui was seen tampering with. I supposed it couldn't hurt to snoop around to see if I could find out anything more.

"Can you describe the men you overheard?" I asked.

"Not really. I peeked out the door, but I didn't want them to know I was listening to them. I'd hoped they'd say more. Both men were about six feet tall, give or take a couple of inches, and both had brown hair. I didn't get a good look at their faces, but one of them had on a pink polo shirt. A very pink shirt," Ellie emphasized.

I was pretty sure I knew who she was referring to. I didn't know his name, but I remembered the pink shirt from the parade. He was driving a blue Cadillac.

"Anything else?" I asked.

"Sorry. I really only caught the tail end of their conversation. They came in from the outside and were talking as they walked. I heard the comment about Jaqui, peeked out the door, and then they turned and walked away."

"Thanks for telling me what you heard. I'll see if I can dig up additional information."

"Did you ever track down Pepper?" Ellie asked as I turned to leave.

"Sort of."

I looked around. The kitchen was empty at the moment, although people had been coming in and out, bringing in empty trays to refill.

"I can't talk here, but if you get a break, we can take a walk and I'll fill you in."

"I can take a break when I finish this. Maybe twenty minutes?"

"I'll let Zak know what we're doing, so just come and find me."

After I left the kitchen, I went in search of Zak. The community center was filled with guys who all sort of looked the same with their slicked-back hair, white T-shirts, and jeans. Of course, Zak was taller than most of the men, so I looked for his slicked-back blond hair. I noticed Scott and Tiffany dancing, so Zak had obviously moved on from him. My dad was twirling my mom around in a circle as several other couples twisted around them. It looked like everyone was having a good time.

"You seen Pandora?" Rizo walked up and asked me. She didn't have on a costume, but she did have her hair in pigtails and was smacking her bubblegum like there was no tomorrow.

"I don't think she was planning to come," I informed her. "She's had a really hard couple of days with everything that's happened."

"She seemed okay at the derby. Did anything happen?"

"No, she just said she was tired."

"Boomer here?" Rizo blew a huge bubble that I was afraid would become a permanent part of her hairdo.

"No, I believe he opted out as well."

Rizo shrugged. "'Kay, just wanted to say 'bye. Guess I'm gonna take off."

"The awards ceremonies are tomorrow," I pointed out.

"Got knocked out of the derby and doubt I won any of the best contests, so I figured I'd blow out early."

The best contests Rizo was referring to were best overall, best modified, best original, best muscle car, and about twenty others. Rizo was probably correct in believing her low-dollar car wouldn't be competitive in any of the categories.

"Okay, well, thanks for participating and I hope to see you next year."

"Toodles." She waved as she skipped away.

I went back to searching for Zak. He didn't seem to be anywhere I could see. Perhaps he'd gone outside. I decided to take a quick look before Ellie came hunting for me.

The patio area was mostly deserted, except for one man who was smoking a cigarette. Luck must have been with me because I was certain he was the man with the pink shirt Ellie had been referring to.

"Nice evening," I said.

"Yeah. It's a lot cooler out here than it is inside that sauna."

"It had gotten a little stuffy with all those dancing bodies. How'd you do in the competition?"

I didn't really care, but I needed to buy some time until I could figure out a way to bring up Jaqui and the night before the race.

"Pretty sure I nailed at least two of the categories. If I win, I'm going to sell the money pit and start over with something new."

"Wouldn't starting over be even more expensive?" I asked.

The man took a long draw of his cigarette and slowly blew the smoke into my face.

Ew.

I tried not to cough as I waited for his reply.

"Yeah," he finally drawled. "More expensive, but a lot more fun."

He inhaled once again. There was no way I was going to stick around for another lungful of secondhand smoke.

"You seen Jaqui?" I asked, hoping to segue into a question about her presence in the garage some of the cars had been kept in after I'd got him talking about the woman.

"Yeah, she just walked by."

"She did?"

Funny; I hadn't seen her all night.

"What did she have on?" I asked.

The man described the exact outfit Rizo was wearing.

"That wasn't Jaqui; that was Rizo."

The man laughed. "I always get those two dames mixed up. Anyway, she went that way."

He pointed toward the garage.

"Okay, thanks. Have a nice evening."

Even as I walked toward the garage, I knew I needed more of a plan than flat out asking Rizo if she'd tampered with Pandora's car. I really should stop to get Zak, but I hated to lose Rizo, and she had said she was going to leave, so I texted him and told him what I was doing. I just hoped he wasn't too preoccupied to check his messages. The last thing I wanted to do was end up almost dead *again.*

"It looks like we're done here," Rizo was saying to a figure wearing dark pants and a dark hooded sweatshirt. The face of the person in black was shielded by the hood, and he or she blended into the dimness of the dark garage.

"I hope everything worked out as planned," Rizo added.

I couldn't hear what the hooded figure said as Rizo was handed a dark gym bag. Rizo unzipped it and peeked inside. She must have been satisfied since she tossed the bag into her car before opening the driver's side door and sliding inside.

She leaned out the window after starting her car. "If you ever need anything else, you know where to find me."

Rizo waved as she exited the garage and sped off down the street.

The person in black faded into the darkness. By the time it occurred to me that I ought to follow him or her, the figure had disappeared into the night.

Chapter 16

Sunday, July 13

After another late night, I was not doing well. I'd called Salinger to fill him in, which earned me the reward of spending most of the evening in his office. When was I ever going to learn to stay out of things? He put out an APB on Rizo, but so far he hadn't been able to track her down. Out of all the possible suspects, Rizo had been the one I'd suspected the least of being the mastermind behind the accident and Isabelle's death. She was such a ditz! Though, when I thought about it, acting like a ditz was the perfect cover.

I had to wonder who the figure in black was and why this person wanted Isabelle dead. And did this person even know that Dezee was Isabelle? I also wondered if Pepper's kidnapping was related or simply a coincidence. There were still a lot of unanswered questions, and to be honest, the whole thing was making me nuts.

The clock was nearing the 2 a.m. mark when Salinger finally got the call he'd been waiting for. I could tell by his frown that we weren't in for a satisfying end to our late-night marathon.

"You're kidding?" He put his head down on his desk after hanging up the phone.

"What?" I asked. We'd been waiting for a call from one of Salinger's deputies regarding a possible Rizo sighting, and I figured that even if they hadn't been able to track her down as we hoped, Salinger wouldn't have been that upset by it.

"It wasn't my men calling about Rizo. It was a friend of mine who confirmed that Stella Worthington's father paid the twenty-million-dollar ransom the kidnappers asked for. When he showed up at the location the kidnappers indicated, Stella was supposed to be waiting for him, but there was no one there."

"You're kidding?" I repeated. "Who called you?"

"A friend of mine who's a PI in New York. He's been keeping an unofficial eye on the situation. The Worthingtons didn't want police interference, but I couldn't quite make myself walk away completely."

"Why New York?"

"That's where the Worthingtons live. My contact was able to tap into a phone line and has been listening from the sidelines."

I had to admit I was surprised that Salinger cared enough to follow up on the kidnapping. When I'd talked to him earlier, he'd seemed happy to wash his hands of the whole thing. I found that his concern for Pepper and her family made me like him a little bit more. Not that having warm feelings for Salinger was sitting well with me. I'd disliked him too intensely for too long to make the leap from resentment to friendship in one giant step, but little by little, as we continued to work together, I found my heart warming up to the toad.

"So what now?" I asked.

"I'm not sure there is anything we can do. Mr. Worthington still hasn't requested police help, and for all we know, Ms. Worthington isn't even in the state any longer."

Talk about frustrating.

"Did you get a hold of Isabelle's dad?"

"I did. He's on his way to identify the body. Not that there's much to identify, but he might know something we don't. All we can do now is wait. You're free to go."

I stood up. "You'll call if you hear anything?"

"I will."

The only bright spot in my day was that the events scheduled for Sunday started much later and ended much earlier than the other days. I was totally exhausted as I made my way to the awards ceremony in the park, but at least I could see the light at the end of the tunnel. I still hadn't heard anything from Salinger, but truth be told, I was almost too tired to care.

Levi and I were scheduled to present the trophy for the derby, while my dad and Paul were to present the awards for all the best categories. Pandora and Boomer looked as tired as I felt. After I'd found out that Pepper hadn't been released by her kidnappers, I'd texted Pandora and filled her in on the turn of events. I could see that she was upset about her friend, but like me, she didn't have any idea what she could do to help.

"The trophies for first and second place are displayed on the table behind the microphone," Hazel informed me.

I yawned.

"If you aren't up to it, I can ask someone else to present." Hazel looked worried. Not that I blamed her. I must look a mess.

"It's okay. I can handle it."

"Levi has already taken his seat, so we can start as soon as Paul gets here. Hopefully it won't take too long. You look like you've been through the ringer."

"It's been a long night," I confirmed.

I made my way over to the bandstand and took my seat next to Levi. I was concentrating on staying awake when I noticed someone lingering on the edge of the area that had been cordoned off for the crowd. The spectator had on black pants and a black hoodie, not really appropriate attire for a summer day.

"I need to check something out," I whispered to Levi. "If they start before I get back, tell Willa I was feeling sick and make the presentation without me."

"Where are you going?" Levi asked.

"I'll tell you when I get back."

I got up, hopped off the bandstand, and made my way through the crowd. By the time I got to the spot where I'd seen the spectator, he or she was gone. I wandered to the edge of the forest surrounding the park and looked around. He couldn't have gotten far. I saw a flash of something in the distance and headed in that direction. By the time I realized what I was doing, I was well away from the safety of the crowd.

I knew the forest like the back of my hand, so I wasn't concerned about getting lost, but after everything that had happened that weekend, I was feeling a significant level of apprehension. Someone had drugged Pandora, tampered with her car, killed Dezee, and kidnapped Pepper, though the last didn't appear to be connected with the car crash, which was absurd because it meant that we had not one but two bad guys. It seemed as if Rizo had been hired to tamper with Pandora's car, although I didn't really *know* that the gym bag contained money.

I was beginning to second-guess my impulse to take off into the forest on my own and was considering whether it would be wiser to turn around when someone grabbed me from behind and wedged a knife up under my chin.

"What are you doing following us?" a voice asked.

"I wasn't following you," I tried.

"Then what are you doing wandering around out here?" The knife dug deeper into my skin.

My instinct told me to struggle, but the more I did, the more force my captor put on my throat.

The best answer I could come up with was a lie that had turned into the truth. "I'm feeling sick and needed to get some air," I answered.

"It's okay." Pepper stepped out from behind some shrubbery. "She won't tell."

"We can't take the chance," the person with the knife said.

"Zoe, are you going to tell anyone you saw me?" Pepper asked.

"No," I gasped. Tears were streaming down my face as the pressure of the knife impeded my ability to breathe properly.

"You're taking a big risk." The person behind me lowered the knife but didn't release the tight hold on me.

"Come on, Izzy. It'll be fine."

Izzy?

"Isabelle?" I took a shot.

Isabelle let go of me and took a step back. I turned around and looked into the face of the man I'd known as Dezee.

"I thought you were dead."

I rubbed my neck, which, thankfully, wasn't bleeding.

"As far as everyone else is concerned I am, and I'd like to stay that way," Isabelle warned me.

"But I saw your body. Everyone did."

"I told you we should never have come back." Isabelle was ignoring me and speaking to Pepper.

"I needed to explain to Pandora." Pepper bit her lip and looked at me with an uncertain expression. She turned back toward Isabelle. "You were right. We should have waited."

"Explained what?" I wondered.

Isabelle raised her knife in a threatening manner. "If you tell anyone . . ."

"I won't," I promised.

I looked at Pepper and then back at Isabelle. Both were dressed in black. Neither spoke.

"Your father thinks you're dead," I said to Isabelle. "He's on his way to identify your body."

"And he will."

I frowned. She seemed fairly certain.

"He knows you're alive?" I guessed.

Pepper took a step forward. "Although we don't know each other well, I feel like I know you well enough to trust you."

"You can," I promised.

"The more people who know what's *really* going on, the more we put ourselves at risk," Isabelle cautioned.

"Let me guess," I began. "The two of you are in love. You've been since Stella was in high school. After Stella's parents found out about the two of you, they fired Isabelle and sent her away. You tried to forget her," I said, turning to Pepper, "but you found that her face haunted your every dream, so you left home and went in search of your one true love."

"A little melodramatic, but you're basically correct." Pepper smiled.

"But you," I looked at Isabelle, "thought that Stella would be better off without you, so you decided that you wouldn't be found. You were as determined to stay gone as Stella was determined to find you."

"Good guess," Pepper confirmed. "Really good. How do you know all of this?"

I blushed. I didn't want to admit that we had read Stella's diary, so I ignored the question and continued speaking.

"At some point I'm guessing you either ran into each other or Isabelle had a change of heart about being found and you reunited. By this point," I said to Pepper, "you were working for Pandora, and you knew that if your parents found out that you and Isabelle had reunited, they'd make trouble for you, so Isabelle became Dezee."

"Actually, my parents didn't know where I was," Pepper informed me. "We were afraid that they were watching Isabelle in order to find me, so she disappeared as well."

I had to hand it to these women; they'd thought this through.

"I assume that you're behind your own kidnapping," I told her. "You figured that faking a ransom demand was the only way to get the money you feel your parents owe you *and* keep Isabelle in your life."

"My grandmother left me money in a trust that I couldn't access without my parents' consent. I only took a small part of what was mine," Pepper defended herself.

That made sense.

"I suppose the two of you plan to use the money to start a life somewhere away from the scrutiny of your parents. There's just one thing I want to know: who died in the crash?"

Isabelle looked at Pepper, who nodded.

"No one," Isabelle informed me.

"We have a body," I reminded them.

"The body in the crash was already dead," Isabelle said. "I drove the car and faked the crash. When the car went around the corner and out of sight, I jumped out. By the time the car had finished burning, there was no way to piece together the fact that the body had actually been on the floor on the passenger side to begin with."

"So the whole thing was planned from the beginning," I realized.

"We needed to find a way to disappear. Isabelle is dead in the morgue and will be positively identified by her dad, and my parents will get proof that I was eliminated by my kidnappers. It was the only way to finally be together without looking over our shoulders all the time."

"Only way? You're both adults. You're in love. I doubt your parents could keep you away from each other no matter how rich and powerful they are."

"During the year between graduation and my running away to join up with Pandora, my parents kept me drugged and locked up," Pepper informed me. "It's only a fluke that I managed to get away. I'm the key that links them to my grandmother's fortune, and they need to control me to maintain control of the money."

"They locked you up?"

"They claimed I was suicidal and delusional. They got some fancy doctor to confirm that I was mentally disturbed and therefore unable to make my own decisions. I was committed to a mental hospital for fourteen long months. I tried to make my doctors understand that I wasn't psychotic, but they wouldn't listen."

"My God," I gasped. "How did you get away?"

"There was a fire, and in the confusion I managed to slip away. I didn't have money or a place to stay, but luckily, I ran into Pandora and she helped me. I became Pepper, and for several years I was off the radar of my powerful family. Then, four months ago, my dad somehow found out where I was. He's been trying to have me forcefully brought to the family ever since."

"So you figured if you were dead, you could finally be free?"

"Exactly."

I took a moment to try to sort through everything the pair was telling me. It all made sense in a convoluted sort of way, except, "Like I asked before, whose body is lying in the morgue?"

"We aren't sure," Pepper admitted. "We purchased the body from a reliable source whose father owns a mortuary. She assured me that no foul play was involved in providing the body and that there would be no grieving relative wondering what had happened to their loved one."

Rizo, I realized.

"And you drugged Pandora?"

"I had to," Pepper confirmed. "I wanted to just tell her what we were doing, but she loved that car, and Isabelle wasn't sure she'd go along with it."

"Why use her car?" I asked.

"The story had to be believable."

"But Pandora and Boomer didn't even decide to have the race until Wednesday afternoon. How could you have pulled this all together that quickly?" I asked.

"Dezee suggested to Boomer that a road race would be a good way to decide the matter of the grouping for the derby before they even met for lunch, and we knew that if Boomer suggested a race, Pandora would never back down. They're both so competitive."

"Okay, last question, I think: why not just let your parents have control of your money in return for letting you live your own life? Why go to the extreme of disappearing off the face of the earth?"

"Because there's one thing my dad cares about more than money: his reputation. He would never have allowed Isabelle and me to be together."

"Because she's a woman?"

"Because she was an employee."

Wow; I have to say I wasn't expecting that.

"I really think I have to agree with Isabelle," I said to Pepper. "I know you want to talk to Pandora, but the police are looking for Rizo. They think she drugged Pandora and killed Dezee. I'm sure it will sort itself out, but in the meantime they're keeping an eye on Pandora in case Rizo tries again."

"I don't want her to worry any more than she already has," Pepper said. "She's been so nice to me."

"I'll fill her in when I get a chance, and you can arrange to meet up with her when everything settles down a bit."

"Will you give this to her?" Pepper handed me an envelope. "It's for the car."

"I'd be happy to."

Pepper hugged me.

"And if Rizo can't work things out with the police, let me know. I don't want her to get in trouble for murder," Pepper added.

"I'll talk to Salinger and tell him I was mistaken about what I saw. Is there a way I can get hold of you if I absolutely need to?"

Pepper looked at Isabelle.

"If you really need to speak to us, call my dad," Isabelle suggested. "He'll know how to reach us."

Isabelle typed a number into my phone.

"It looks like your cute friend is heading this way," Pepper commented.

I turned around and saw that Levi was heading in our direction. I doubted he could see us yet since we were shielded by a grove of trees, but it wouldn't be long.

Pepper hugged me one more time, then faded into the dense cover of the forest.

"What are you doing all the way out here?" Levi asked.

"You're never going to believe it."

Chapter 17

Monday, July 14

Fate is a strange thing. After a week of agonizing over giving Zak an answer to his proposal, I was finally ready to say yes. Sure, I was scared, and my stomach felt like a full-on hurricane was going on inside, but I knew I loved Zak and I knew I wanted to be his wife. I'm not sure why the idea of marriage freaked me out the way it did, but I tried to imagine a life without Zak and realized that was a possibility I didn't even want to toy with.

Levi had taken Scooter fishing and they would be gone most of the day. Zak had originally planned to go with them but then ended up having some sort of important conference call to deal with. I was sorry Zak appeared to be getting involved in another of his projects since they tended to pull him away from Aston Falls, but I was thrilled he missed the fishing trip because it meant we'd have the entire day all to ourselves.

I'd dressed in my favorite sundress and even took care with my hair and makeup. After all, you only get engaged once. I tried to imagine how it would feel to be someone's fiancée. Zak's fiancée.

I'd never been the type of little girl to play wedding or spend hours imagining how my prince charming would sweep me off my feet. I hadn't thought I'd want some big ceremony, but watching my parents as they planned their own event caused me to pause and consider the possibility of a grand affair with all my friends in attendance to witness the most important moment of my life.

I put the dogs out into the yard before going in search of Zak. I found him in his living room, talking to someone on the phone.

"I have news," I said as soon as he hung up.

"Me too." He beamed.

"You first," I insisted. I didn't want anything except long hours of lovemaking to come after my own announcement.

"Are you sure?" Zak looked uncertain. "I didn't mean to upstage your announcement."

"I'm sure," I insisted as my stomach continued to churn in anticipation. "What's up?"

Zak put his hands on my shoulders and looked directly into my eyes. "I've just been notified that I've been chosen as number four on *Whose Who* magazine's ten most eligible bachelors list."

"Wow." I was pretty sure I was going to pass out. "Number four," I added weakly.

Zak frowned. "You seem disappointed."

"No," I assured him. "I'm very happy for you, but you clearly should have been number one."

I hugged Zak and tried to mask my disappointment at the timing of his news.

"Congratulations. Really," I added as I kissed Zak.

"I know it's silly, and I'm as surprised as anyone that I even care, but somehow when they told me I made the list, I was really jazzed. Besides, it'll be good publicity for the new software company I'm thinking of launching."

"You're thinking of launching a new company?"

I needed to sit down. I knew Zak was working on a project, but he'd never mentioned that he had plans to get into a new *company*. I'd hoped we'd have more time together now that the project he'd been working on since the previous fall had finally been wrapped up.

"A friend of mine approached me before we left for Maui, but I had an idea that perhaps I was going to spend the next year focusing on something other than software, so I told him I wasn't interested. But he called again after I got home, and we had a really long talk. It looks like my original plan might not pan out after all, so I told him I'd be interested in talking specifics. It's not like I can sit around and do nothing forever, and this really is a good opportunity."

My face fell. I imagined the plans that had fallen through were *marriage plans*. I wanted to set the record straight, but now the timing seemed off.

"We'll need to go to New York for the photo shoot," he continued. "I know you're going to be busy planning your parents' wedding, but they want me there a week from Monday and I really want you to come with me."

"What about Scooter?" I asked.

Zak averted his eyes, the way he does when he's about to ask a favor, which I have to admit doesn't happen very often.

"I figured that if you came with me to New York, we could bring Scooter with us and you could go sightseeing with him while I was tied up."

Sounds romantic.

I was about to flat-out refuse to go along with Zak's babysitting idea when I took a moment to look at Zak's face. In spite of the fact that being named one of the country's most eligible bachelors didn't seem at all like something Zak would be into, he looked happy. It occurred to me that, once again, I was being Selfish Zoe. Sure, my plans had taken a detour, but really, whose fault was that? If I'd said yes to Zak right off, chances were we would be planning a wedding rather than having this discussion.

"I'd love to come," I found myself saying. "Ellie is moving into the boathouse next weekend, so I'm sure she'll be happy to keep an eye on the animals. You can bring Bella over as well."

"Thanks, Zoe." Zak kissed me and I felt myself melt. He really was the best boyfriend.

"So what was your news?" he asked.

Zak looked at me expectantly while I hesitated to answer.

"I just wanted to let you know that my parents finally set a date for their wedding," I found myself saying. "It's going to be August 23."

"That's great." Zak smiled. "It looks like things are working out all around."

Chapter 18

Saturday, August 23

The Wedding

I'm not sure how I thought I'd feel as I watched my parents *finally* become man and wife. I know that this very moment was something I'd been dreaming of since I was old enough to dream. I love them both so much, and deep in my heart, I've always known that they should be together rather than continents apart. Dad looked so handsome in his casual day suit, while Mom was beautiful in her peach-colored dress and stylish hat.

It was a beautiful sunny day and the sky was as blue as I'd ever seen it. Although there was a light breeze to keep things cool, the surface of the lake was perfectly still, like a mirror provided just for the occasion.

Mom's friend Ava helped Hazel with the flowers that transformed Zak's patio area into a garden paradise. Dozens of flowers in peach, white, and yellow were arranged in large displays everywhere that a bare spot provided the opportunity for one of Ava's beautiful bouquets. I hadn't wanted Ellie to have to spend the entire day in the kitchen, so I'd hired a caterer, but as I should have predicted, Ellie was in there keeping an eye on things anyway.

Harper and I were wearing dresses in a soft sea-foam color that perfectly matched the ribbon in Mom's dress. The reception was spectacular, but the service was magical.

Jeremy played a medley of songs my parents picked out as Harper and I, followed by Pappy and Mom, walked down the aisle to join Dad and Zak, who were waiting for us on the temporary platform Zak had built as an extension to his lakeside deck.

As I walked toward Zak, I let myself imagine walking toward him on another day in another place and time. I'm not sure why things worked out the way they have, but I suppose there are things in life that can be rushed and there are others—important things—that demand to wait for their own time. I know deep in my heart that, although it isn't today, one day Zak and I will have our moment.

Dad and Mom elected to write their own vows, which they recited while gazing deeply into the eyes of the other. They had been in love for their entire adult lives, in spite of the decisions they'd made, but as I listened to them declare their feeling for each other, I knew that for once and forever, Mom was finally home.

"It really was a lovely ceremony," Phyllis King, a member of the book club I attend, as well as Jeremy's landlady, commented as I helped Ellie replenish the food, which had been quickly devoured.

"It was perfect," I agreed. "I noticed you held Morgan during the ceremony, while Jeremy was playing the processional."

"I love that little girl and am so very glad that you thought to suggest that Jeremy rent my town house. Jessica is here with Rosalie as well. If you want my opinion, I think Jeremy and Jessica might be having the next wedding."

"Really?" I knew Jeremy and Jessica were friends and suspected their relationship might have developed into something more, but I'd never thought marriage might be on the horizon.

"I suppose my interpretation of the situation may just be the hopes of an old woman, but it seems that Jessica and Rosalie are at the town house more often than not. Jessica babysits Morgan a lot, and Rosalie likes to stop by to see the kitten Jeremy got for her, but if this grandma surrogate has her way, the four of them will be a family by this time next year."

As far as I was concerned, the idea of Jeremy and Jessica marrying had its merits. Jessica was a few years older, but Jeremy really had matured since Morgan was born.

"I noticed Scooter is still here," Phyllis commented.

"Zak managed to get him into a boarding school on the East Coast that we think will work out perfectly for an energetic little boy. Zak and Scooter took a trip to visit the school, and Scooter loved the place. He really was bored living on his grandparents' farm, and we hope that if he's placed in an environment where there's plenty to do to keep him physically and mentally occupied, he'll really flourish. He already met his roommate, and the two boys seemed to hit it off."

"You know, I went to boarding school when I was a child," Phyllis shared.

"I didn't realize that. How did you like it?"

"I *loved* it. My parents were both academics who traveled a lot, and I hated being left with a nanny." Phyllis was a retired English professor who had gone into academia herself. "I suppose that's why I never married and had children of my own. I always felt my parents would have been happier without me to consider."

"I'm sure they loved you." I had no idea whatsoever if Phyllis's parents had loved and wanted her, but it seemed the supportive thing to say.

"Perhaps. I sometime regret the life I chose. Don't misunderstand me: I have many close friends and have traveled more than most, but when I hold little Morgan and think about the experiences I missed out on . . ."

I squeezed Phyllis's hand.

"When does Scooter leave for school?" she asked.

"Zak and I are going to get him settled in next weekend. He starts school after Labor Day."

"That will be nice."

I was looking forward to the trip. Not only were we going to get Scooter settled but we planned to take an extra week to stay at his friend's house in the Hamptons. Just the two of us. No friends, no jobs, no murder investigations (I hoped).

After I spoke to Phyllis, I decided to work my way around the patio. Zak looked very 007 in his suit, and the only thing I really wanted to do was shoo everyone away, but I knew *that* would be rude. Zak hadn't brought up his proposal again after I got distracted by his status as a most eligible bachelor, and I hadn't either. Basically, I had been living with him since Ellie had moved into my boathouse. It really was too small for both of us, so I'd packed up Charlie and the cats and moved in with Zak and Scooter temporarily.

I know Zak wants me to take the leap and move all my stuff over. Now that Ellie is living in the boathouse, I feel better about leaving. She's been marathon dating all summer, and I know she enjoys having her own place to come back to, especially since she's *seemed* to have found just the right guy right here in Ashton Falls. I suppose time will tell if he actually is the right one, but he's nice and easygoing, never married, and seems open to the idea of a big family.

"Beautiful wedding." Tiffany kissed me on the cheek.

"Thanks. It really was nice. Is Scott here?"

"Yeah. He's talking to Jeremy about the mountain lion that was brought in yesterday. It seems like it's always work, work, work with him, but I love it. Are your parents going on a honeymoon?"

"They're going to Paris for a month," I informed her. "They're taking Harper with them, and Pappy is going to stay at their house and take care of the dogs and the store."

"Paris." Tiffany got a dreamy look in her eyes. "Have they been before?"

"Mom has, but Dad hasn't. I'm sure they'll have a blast."

"Are you ready for your own trip?" Tiffany asked.

"Almost."

"Need a babysitter for the cats?" Tiffany asked hopefully.

I knew Tiffany had enjoyed her time with Marlow and Spade when we were in Maui.

"I was going to ask Ellie, but actually, if you wouldn't mind staying at Zak's, that might be very helpful."

"Seriously?" Tiffany gasped. "You want me to stay in Zak's mansion?"

"Ellie has been living in the boathouse, so I've been staying here and have already moved the cats over. We're taking Charlie with us but leaving Bella, so you'd have to watch her as well, but you could bring her to the Zoo during the day so she won't have to be alone. Actually, if you're willing to stay here, it would be a huge help."

Tiffany hugged me. "Thank you, thank you. This place is great. Lakeside with a pool and a home theater. It really will be like being on vacation, and I'd love to bring Bella to work with me."

I laughed as Tiffany hugged me again. "I'm glad it'll work out for both of us."

"Is it okay if I have Scott over for a romantic dinner?"

"Absolutely. I'll get you all set up in one of the guest rooms."

I looked toward where Bella and Charlie were napping in the shade. I was glad Tiffany had volunteered. Ellie would have been happy to do it, but with her working all day, I was worried that Bella would get lonely.

"Any time you need a house sitter, I'm your girl," Tiffany assured me.

"Zak and I may have to go to Ireland after the holidays. You know he started that new company?"

"I'd heard. Is it going well?"

"Really well, although there'll be a fair amount of travel, and I'll feel better about tagging along if I know that Bella and the cats are well tended to."

"Count me in," Tiffany said enthusiastically.

"It looks like my mom is waving at me to come over and talk with her parents before they leave," I informed Tiffany.

"Leave? The reception just got started."

I looked toward the stodgy couple dressed in black. They looked like they were dressed to attend a funeral, not an outdoor wedding. I suspected their choice of dress had been intentional. They'd never approved of my dad and were the people behind my mother leaving me with him in the first place.

"Yeah, well, they really aren't as thrilled about the marriage as everyone else. In fact, I'm surprised they came at all."

"You aren't close to your grandparents?" Tiffany frowned.

"We don't really know each other," I said. "I met them a few times when I was a child, but the only real memory I have of our time together is being terrified that I'd do something wrong."

"Wow. That's too bad."

"Yeah. I guess that not having a relationship with their granddaughters is their choice."

"Well, they're the ones missing out. You're both awesome."

"Yeah." I smiled. "We are."

After I said my good-byes to my grandparents and watched them drive away in their huge limo, I went in search of the grandparent who loved me and *had* been part of my life. Pappy was talking to Nick, Hazel, and a couple of other members of our book club. He smiled and put an arm around me when I walked over to join them. He knows that the fact that my mother's parents don't seem to care a bit about me hurts me, even though I try to tell myself it doesn't. Unlike the Montgomerys, Pappy has been a loving part of my everyday life from the day Mom dropped me off on Dad's doorstep.

"So who's the girl with Levi?" Pappy asked.

Nick and Hazel seemed interested in the answer as well.

"Her name is Darla. She moved to Ashton Falls to work with Serenity after Barbie left town."

"Another yoga instructor?" Hazel asked with a look of disapproval. "Didn't that boy learn his lesson with the last one?"

I shrugged. "I guess he likes them bendy, and Darla seems nice. She has the whole serene-lover-of-all-living-things vibe going on like Serenity, rather than the sexy-lover-of-all-men vibe Barbie had. They haven't been dating long, so who knows if the relationship will amount to anything, but so far I like her."

"I guess you heard about the debacle with the Haunted Hamlet," Hazel said, changing the subject.

"Debacle? What debacle?"

I was in charge of the event this year and didn't want anything to interfere with my time away with Zak. The Haunted Hamlet was still almost two months away, but I knew from past experience what a huge time suck the events we sponsored could be if even one little thing went wrong.

"It's not the haunted maze?" I groaned. The landowner who'd let us use his field last year had complained about the noise and damage.

"No, not the maze. The haunted barn," Hazel informed me.

"What?" The haunted barn had been held in the same deserted barn since I was a child.

"The property was sold as part of an estate sale and the new owner is using the barn as an actual home for his livestock. We'll need to find another venue."

That wasn't going to be easy. It wasn't like there were a lot of deserted buildings around town. The barn had been perfect. The fact that it was old and deserted gave the event an authentic feel.

"Any ideas?" I asked.

"Not a one." Hazel confirmed what I already expected.

"We could just decorate the community center," Nick suggested.

We could. A lot of towns did just that, but somehow I didn't think that a dressed-up community center would provide the spook factor the barn had.

"Don't worry." Pappy put his arm around me. "We have time to figure something out. For now, you should enjoy the reception."

I looked over at Mom and Dad, who were talking to Jeremy, Jessica, and Rosalie. Mom was holding Harper, who was laughing at the funny faces Rosalie was making. For the first time in my life, I felt like I was part of a *real* family.

"We did it." Zak walked up behind me and grabbed me around the waist. He pulled me to a location behind a grove of trees where no one could see us. He wrapped me in his arms and kissed my neck.

"Yeah." I turned and wrapped my arms around his waist. "We really did."

Zak tucked a stray lock of my hair behind my ear with the index finger of his right hand.

"It's been a very nice day, but I can't wait to get you alone," he whispered in my ear.

"Everyone should be gone in a few hours."

"I wasn't talking about today," Zak clarified. "I was talking about our trip. Just you," he kissed my lips, "and me," he kissed me again, "in a house by the sea."

I giggled at his lame attempt at poetry, but I agreed with the sentiment. I couldn't wait to get Zak alone with no interruptions.

"Tiffany is going to stay at your house with Bella and the cats," I informed him.

"Sounds good." Zak gently kissed my neck.

"You know that I love you."

"I love you too." He moved his lips around to the back.

"It seems that Ellie has settled into the boathouse," I added.

"Umm," Zak replied as he lowered his lips just a bit.

"I've been thinking about it, and I was wondering if you'd been okay with me moving some more of my stuff over here."

Zak lifted his head and smiled.

"You know you're welcome to bring anything you'd like. What were you thinking?"

"All of it."

Zak grinned. "Really?"

"Really," I screeched as he lifted me into his arms.

"Does this mean what I think it means?" Zak looked into my eyes as he held me against his chest.

"That you're going to get stuck living with a crazy woman."

Zak grinned. "I've been dreaming of crazy since the moment I met crazy."

Recipes for Derby Divas

Buffalo Chicken Appetizer Pizza
Chicken and Rice
White Bean Chili
Easy Vegetarian Black Bean Chili
Hobo Packs
Mocha Ice Cream Pie

Buffalo Chicken Appetizer Pizza

4 tortillas
1 jar alfredo sauce, any brand
4 cups mozzarella cheese, shredded
2 chicken breasts, cooked, cubed, and tossed with Frank's RedHot Buffalo Wing Sauce
1 can artichoke hearts, diced (approx. 14 oz.)
1 can spinach (approx. 14 oz.)
grated Parmesan cheese

Makes 4 servings

For each serving:
I large flour tortilla toasted (I put it on a sandwich grill, but you can toast in oven)

Cover with:
2 tbsp. alfredo sauce (you can use more or less per your taste)
1 cup mozzarella cheese
½ prepared chicken breast
¼ can artichoke hearts
¼ can spinach, squeezed of excess liquid
Sprinkle with grated Parmesan to taste

Bake in 350-degree oven for 15 minutes or until cheese is melted and toppings are heated.

Note: you can leave off the chicken for a vegetarian variety or replace toppings with pepperoni, olives, mushrooms, whatever your taste. You can also replace the alfredo sauce with pizza sauce.

Chicken and Rice

Two variations for twice the fun!

Traditional Chicken and Rice

Combine:

1½ cups Minute rice
2 cans mushroom soup
2 soup cans of milk
2 packets of onion soup mix

Pour into greased 9" x 13" baking dish. Place 3–4 chicken breasts on top. Cover with foil.

Bake for 60 minutes at 350 degrees.

Remove foil and bake uncovered for an additional 20 minutes.

Cheesy Chicken and Rice

Combine:

1½ cups Minute rice
1 can cheddar cheese soup
1 jar alfredo sauce
1 soup can of milk

Pour into greased 9" x 13" baking dish. Place 3–4 chicken breasts on top. Cover with foil.

Bake for 60 minutes at 350 degrees.

Remove foil and bake uncovered for an additional 20 minutes.

Note: sometimes I spread shredded cheddar over the top after I remove foil.

White Bean Chili

4 chicken breasts, cubed

Sauté in olive oil until chicken is cooked through.

Add:

1 onion, diced
2 carrots, diced
2 stalks celery, diced
2 cloves garlic, diced

Sauté until veggies are tender.

Add to chicken mixture:

2 cans Great Northern White Beans
1 can chicken broth
2 cans diced Ortega Green Chilis
1 tsp. salt
1 tsp. cumin
1 tsp. oregano
1 tsp. pepper
1 tsp. cayenne pepper (or more if you like it hot)

Cook over medium heat until warm

Stir in:

1 cup sour cream
½ cup heavy whipping cream

Heat for a few more minutes

Serve with tortillas.

Easy Vegetarian Black Bean Chili

Sauté in small amount of olive oil:

1 bell pepper, diced
1 onion, diced
2 cloves garlic, chopped

Add:

1 tsp. cumin
1 tsp. oregano
2 tsp. chili powder

Add:

1 tub salsa (I use hot, but you can use mild)
1 15 oz. can black beans, drained

Cook on medium heat until warm

Serve with rice and tortillas.

Hobo Packs

Anyone who has ever gone camping has probably made a hobo pack. There are as many variations as there are people making them. Basically, you place your meat and veggies in a large piece of heavy-duty foil and then place the foil in the coals of a hot-burning wood or charcoal fire. You can make many different variations, but my favorite is the basic meat and potato kind.

On a large piece of heavy-duty foil, place:

seasoned hamburger patty
thinly sliced potato
thinly sliced carrot
sliced onion
asparagus spears

Wrap the foil around the food (I double wrap) and place into the coals of the fire, turning occasionally. Cook until desired doneness (this depends on the amount of food and the temperature of the fire).

You can also do this with steak, chicken, fish, and any type of veggie you like.

Mocha Ice Cream Pie

Melt:
3 tbsp. butter in sauce pan

Add:
2 tbsp. brown sugar
¼ cup corn syrup

Cook on medium heat until it boils. Pour over 2½
cups Rice Krispies cereal.

Press into buttered pie plate.

Mix together:
½ cup caramel sauce
½ cup peanut butter
3 tbsp. corn syrup

Spread half on piecrust. Cover with softened coffee
ice cream. Spread other half of sauce mixture on top.
Freeze for 2–3 hours.

Books by Kathi Daley

Come for the murder, stay for the romance.

Buy them on Amazon today.

Zoe Donovan Cozy Mystery:

Halloween Hijinks
The Trouble With Turkeys
Christmas Crazy
Cupid's Curse
Big Bunny Bump-off
Beach Blanket Barbie
Maui Madness
Derby Divas
Haunted Hamlet
Turkeys, Tuxes, and Tabbies
Christmas Cozy
Alaskan Alliance
Shamrock Shenanigans – March 2015

Paradise Lake Cozy Mystery:

Pumpkins in Paradise
Snowmen in Paradise
Bikinis in Paradise
Christmas in Paradise

Puppies in Paradise – February 2015

Whales and Tails Cozy Mystery:
Romeow and Juliet – January 2015

Road to Christmas Romance:
Road to Christmas Past

Kathi Daley lives with her husband, kids, grandkids, and Bernese mountain dogs in beautiful Lake Tahoe. When she isn't writing, she likes to read (preferably at the beach or by the fire), cook (preferably something with chocolate or cheese), and garden (planting and planning, not weeding). She also enjoys spending time on the water when she's not hiking, biking, or snowshoeing the miles of desolate trails surrounding her home.

Kathi uses the mountain setting in which she lives, along with the animals (wild and domestic) that share her home, as inspiration for her cozy mysteries.

Stay up to date with her newsletter, *The Daley Weekly*. There's a link to sign up on both her Facebook page and her website, or you can access the sign-in sheet at: http://eepurl.com/NRPDf

Visit Kathi:

Facebook at Kathi Daley Books, www.facebook.com/kathidaleybooks

Twitter at Kathi Daley@kathidaley

Webpage www.kathidaley.com

E-mail kathidaley@kathidaley.com

CPSIA information can be obtained
at www.ICGtesting.com
Printed in the USA
FSHW020234191218
54525FS